RAINBOW AND MR ZED

RAINBOW
AND MR ZED

The Sequel to Ultramarine

Jenny Nimmo

METHUEN

First published in 1992
by Methuen Children's Books
A Division of Reed International Books Ltd
Michelin House, 81 Fulham Road, London SW3 6RB
Copyright © 1992 Jenny Nimmo
Printed and bound in Great Britain by
Butler & Tanner Ltd, Frome and London

A CIP catalogue for this title
is available from the British Library

ISBN 0 416 17222 9

For Harriet and Lydia

Contents

ONE

The Footsteps Fade

When Nell stood near her brother she could hear the ocean. It was not the whispered rustling that can be heard in a shell; and it was not the drone of waves on the seashore near their home. It was a little echo of footsteps moving through water and it did not come from inside Ned, exactly, but his presence made it happen. The sound kept Nell afloat.

For Nell had a tendency to sink. She quickly became despondent about school-work, about the way she looked, about pollution and the suffering of animals.

Now her brother, Ned, was a thousand miles away. It was their first holiday apart and Nell must learn to keep afloat without him. So she had fixed a smile on her face, to show that she was a confident, outgoing sort of girl with happy thoughts, hoping that she would grow to match her new expression. But in her mirror the smile looked fraudulent and lopsided and certainly didn't fool her.

A girl peeped into Nell's bedroom. 'Are you ready?' she asked. She was smaller than Nell and her head was crowned with dark glossy curls. Her name was Menna.

'I think so,' Nell said, holding on to the smile. She was about to spend two weeks with Menna and her parents in the family beach-house further down the coast.

'Is that all you're taking?' Menna eyed the meagre lumps in a red rucksack that lay on Nell's bed.

'I don't need much,' Nell said. No one had properly explained to her what she would be doing. Leah, her stepmother, often forgot about the things that did not seem to matter as much as love and hugs. And Mark, her stepfather, had only told her that she would be with his sister and, therefore, quite safe. 'We won't be going anywhere smart, will we?' Nell asked Menna, suddenly alerted to possible visits with even more new relations.

Menna shrugged. 'Not that I know of. The house is right on the beach, closer to the sea than yours. We'll be swimming and windsurfing and maybe scuba diving. We've got all the gear.'

'Oh,' murmured Nell, her voice sounding rather forlorn. She took one last look around the room she had grown up in, very tidy now without the usual clutter of pencils and school work; her shells safely hidden in marked boxes, her books and toys stacked neatly in a cupboard.

'Come on!' In an instant Menna had bounced into the room and seized the rucksack.

'Careful,' Nell said timidly. 'There are things in there that might break.' She did not mention the treasured necklace that lay curled in a box at the top of her rucksack.

'Sorry,' Menna grinned.

And Nell thought she might learn to be friends with this small confident girl, but it would not be easy. She had hoped that Menna would be shy and a little unsure, like herself, and that they would unfold gradually and find they shared the same outlook. But it would not be like that. Menna was obviously an accomplished water athlete. There were many things Nell would have to learn. A knot formed in her stomach, and the trick-smile wouldn't come.

As they went downstairs, Leah emerged from the kitchen still talking to Menna's mother, Anne. She had hair like Menna's and a friendly brown-eyed face.

They're getting on all right, Nell thought, so maybe there's a chance for me and Menna. She applied her full-bodied smile, hoping that these two step-relations would feel comfortable with her.

Leah flung an arm round Nell; Mark hugged them both. There were kisses on Nell's cheeks and she held back the tears, but Leah was crying for her; Leah could cry with happiness and Nell knew that her stepmother's eyes were really sparkling with pride. She knew the giant step Nell was taking.

They were on the way to a blue station wagon. It was all going too fast. There was something Nell must say, now, before it was too late. But they were moving in a hurried bunch and she couldn't remember what it was.

'We'll take care of her,' Anne cried in a hearty voice.

'Could I have my bag with me?' Nell said, to Menna, who was about to sling the rucksack into the boot.

''Course,' Menna handed it over.

'We'll phone when we arrive,' Anne Parry announced, settling herself behind the wheel. 'Climb in, girls!'

Menna opened a door for Nell, who sidled in, away from her family. She raised a hand to them, still holding the smile, but Menna was in the way. The car began to move and Nell waved over her shoulder. She didn't want Menna to guess that it was the first time she had ever left home.

Anne made friendly enquiries about the town as they travelled along the seafront and then she fell silent, concentrating on motorway directions. Menna clamped a pair of earphones to her head and switched on a cassette-player clipped to her jeans. Nell gazed helplessly at the receding cluster of buildings and clutched her rucksack. She could feel the sharp corners of the box that held her necklace and the ghost of her true smile crept into her eyes.

It was almost dusk when they arrived. The Parrys' beach-house was just as Menna had described, nearly in the sea; a humped grey house, built with wood and roofed in dark slate. It had a balcony half-way up that ringed the house like the brim of a trilby hat, and the salt-scarred paint gave the walls a cracked-egg look.

They parked at the edge of the dunes and Menna and her mother began to walk down the track that led to the house. Nell took a deep breath. The Parrys had not waited for her so there was no one to see her stealthy drink of sea air.

She was about to follow the others when something caught her eye. Beyond the weatherworn building a light glimmered far, far away. It was so faint Nell had the impression that she was seeing an image printed on the wind not the real light at all. And hiding in the sounds that blew off the sea there were voices, almost indistinguishable from waves and bird calls, but voices all the same. And although Nell could not make out any words she knew they were trapped in the light that spun into the thundery sky, and she found that she was crying.

'Nell, what is it, dear?' Anne had turned back for her. 'We'll ring Leah, shall we? And then Menna wants to show you everything before dark.' A hand rested on Nell's arm gently leading her forward.

'What's out there?' asked Nell, pointing to a hollow in the clouds where the faint sparkle had suddenly vanished.

'Where?' Anne frowned into the wind. 'There's only the sea, Nell.'

'There it is,' Nell nodded as another faraway beam glinted through the clouds. 'Is it a lighthouse?' She did not believe this because of the voices. She knew it had to be something more mysterious, but she did not mention the voices because she knew they did not reach Anne, who had a homespun look, and would never admit ghostly things into her life – even if she saw them.

'The only thing out there is Mr Zed's island,' Anne said. 'But I don't see any light. The island is miles and miles away, far beyond the horizon. It's right out in the Atlantic.'

'Mr Zed?' Nell repeated the name, wondering why it

struck a little chord in her mind.

They had reached a large window where warm lights revealed a room that glowed with faded cushions and golden wicker furniture.

'Who is Mr Zed?' Nell whispered as Anne opened a door stripped of colour by the salt wind.

'That's a good question,' Anne said, drawing Nell through the door. It opened directly into the room with wicker furniture.

'Here we are!' welcomed Menna, bouncing on faded cushions while tired springs clanged beneath her.

'Menna, careful, love. Let's keep the sofa going one more year,' sighed Anne.

'We'll go and unpack,' yelled Menna, her earphones dancing round her neck. She grabbed Nell's rucksack and leapt up the bare boards of a contrary sort of staircase with steps that didn't match and led you round and round, deceiving you with unexpected variations in depth.

Nell wondered when she could make the promised phone call but did not like to mention it. She stumbled after Menna tripping on steps that had mysteriously grown an inch and stamping on ones that had shrunk, until she found herself on a landing with three doors before her and one beside. The centre door was open.

'We've got the best room,' Menna shouted from the room beyond, 'because there are two of us.'

Nell stepped inside and found herself facing a large window filled with a dark grey mass of sea. Menna sprawled on a bed behind the door, the other bed, beside the window, was smoothly inviting with its quilted rectangle of flowers. Yet Nell hesitated, a bed beside the ocean was too much to hope for.

'Sorry,' Menna grinned. 'You've got the one that gets wet; only when it rains, though, and it might never rain. When it does – wow! The wind comes off the sea and fairly shakes the old place; water pours through gaps in the gutters and tips into the rattly windows like

13

nothing you'd believe. That's why we can never come here in winter.' She accompanied this speech with dramatic gestures, clearly enjoying herself.

'I don't mind,' Nell said disappointingly. She went to claim her bed, sitting on it and hugging the rucksack with her curious false smile.

'Let's empty our bags!' Menna did everything in a fierce sort of rush. Now she leapt off the bed and from an upended black bag shook out an assortment of clothes, books and bags that had all been squashed higgledy-piggledy together. She strewed these items all over her quilt as though she were sowing seeds. The effect was unsatisfactory and she turned hopefully to Nell, demanding, 'What have you brought?'

'Not much,' Nell said guardedly.

'Let's have a look!' Menna seized the red bag but Nell clutched the strap and cried angrily, 'Leave it!'

'OK.' Menna backed off. 'Sorry!' She slumped on her bed making Nell feel mean and foolish, but she didn't know how to unpack without revealing the necklace. She unzipped the bag and laid out her small wardrobe, taking care to keep the box out of sight.

'I like your sweater,' said Menna edging toward friendliness.

Nell had to match her effort, somehow. She needed Menna to be friends. Her hand was still on the box. She drew it toward her, opened it and held it out to Menna.

'Wow!' Menna gazed at the strand of shells and stones glimmering in its velvet nest. 'I've never seen any of those shells.' She touched the crystal threaded in the centre of the necklace. 'And this one's like a sort of diamond, but it feels so – old; I don't know why.' She shivered and wrapped her arms round herself. 'It makes me think of icy places where no one's ever been. Where did it come from?'

'My father made the necklace for me,' Nell said without pride. 'And the shells, they come from the furthest ocean.'

14

'Which is that?' asked Menna practically.

'I suppose it depends where you're going from,' said Nell.

'The Arctic, I bet,' said Menna. 'Or the Indian. Is it the Pacific? It can't be the Atlantic because there it is, right on our doorsteps, and not far away at all.'

Nell could not explain that her father's furthest ocean was not on any map but a region that was without definition; a vast never-ending sweep of sea that lay beyond their reach. That's how he had described it. 'I don't know its name,' she said, 'but it's where kelpies are born.'

'Kelpies, what are they?' In one of her sudden bursts of energy, Menna bounced over to Nell and drew her down on to the bed beside her.

'Kelpies,' answered Nell, 'look like men, sometimes; in fact they *are* men, sometimes but . . .'

'They're mermen, I suppose,' Menna gave a hearty laugh. 'Men with fish tails like mermaids.'

'Not like that at all,' said Nell in a shocked voice. 'They're . . .'

Menna did not interrupt but merely drummed her fingers on her knees in what she hoped was an encouragement to this strange girl who took so long to reveal things.

'Well, people used to think they were water demons,' Nell said, falling back on the well-worn description. 'They said they lured maidens into lakes and estuaries, promising them love and marriage, and then drowned them.'

'But you don't believe that,' Menna said, perceptively.

'It's just not true,' Nell told her vehemently. 'Kelpies save things, they don't drown them.'

For the first time since they had met, Menna looked thoughtful. With surprising gentleness she touched the necklace that lay on Nell's lap and Nell was almost coaxed into letting more secrets slip out, but Menna

15

spoiled the mood by leaping up and, with a look of irritation, muttering, 'Well, I don't know about all that stuff. Come on!'

So Nell closed the lid on her treasure and slid the box under her pillow, before trailing down the tricky staircase after this boisterous person, who was to be her companion for two whole weeks.

I didn't have to come here, thought Nell. It was my decision so I'd better get on with it. She found her lopsided smile and fixed it on her face, stoically.

'Want to come on the beach?' asked Menna when supper was over.

'OK,' Nell tried to hide the rush of pleasure. She longed to touch the ocean.

'You'll need jackets,' Anne said. 'It's chilly now, and getting dark, so don't go too far.'

Menna flew off as though triggered, while Nell approached the tricky staircase, trying to work out a way of navigating the wayward steps efficiently. Tomorrow, she silently vowed, I'll practise until I'm perfect. As though it were a tune she could memorize.

'It's a horror, isn't it?' called Anne laughing. 'We keep meaning to do something about it. We stumble and fall, knock our shins and rattle our brains and swear to fix it, but in two days our legs have learned its pattern and it seems a shame to tear the old thing down.'

'It would be,' Nell agreed.

Menna met her half-way up, with two anoraks. 'Tomorrow,' she said, 'I expect you to climb up here with your eyes closed. That's how I learned to do it.'

Nell imagined that Menna only enjoyed challenging exercises.

The wind met them at the door. It had churned the sea into a foamy broth. There would be no windsurfing tomorrow if the weather didn't change. Nell found she was relieved. She liked her sea when it was unapproachable and treacherous.

16

A dog leapt out of nowhere, barking at the drifting sand, then bounding after Menna as she raced along the tideline. 'His name is Marshall,' she called. 'He's always on the beach. His owner lives a mile away but she never bothers to come with him.' She swooped back to Nell. 'He loves a chase. There's stuff to throw for him, all along the edge of the sea. It makes you wonder where it comes from.'

'People dump it,' Nell said. 'It floats for miles and miles and kills things on the way.'

'Yes,' said Menna fleetingly subdued. 'I know.' She picked out a chunk of grey wood, shaped like a fish and flung it into the air. With the wind behind it the wooden fish travelled much further than she could have sent it and Marshall, overcome with excitement, bounded across the sand with great joyful yelps.

The girls laughed together and followed the dog, Menna flying before the wind and leaving Nell so far behind she felt she could hardly be moving at all.

When she reached Menna, girl and dog were tussling with the stick. Menna was almost breathless with giggling. 'Take it, quickly,' she cried. 'He's so funny, this dog, he goes mad with a stick.'

Nell grabbed the wooden fish and threw it. Marshall reared up to her hand, twisted in mid-air and was off again with Menna in pursuit, considerably slowed-down by laughter.

Nell smiled and even giggled but this time she didn't follow Menna. She felt a tug from the sea and ambled towards it, squinting at the horizon. There *was* something there and she could hear it, even if it was on the other side of the ocean. It trickled towards her, a teasing sound like a familiar word you try to snatch from the radio before it's lost in the rumble of a thousand languages. She stood very still at the edge of the tide, straining to recognize the call, ready to pounce and hold it.

'What are you doing?' Menna intercepted the voice as

17

it trickled over the ocean and Nell, turning, said fretfully, 'I heard something.'

''Course you did. That old sea's like thunder when it's windy.'

'No. Not the sea.'

'A shipwreck then? An S.O.S?' Menna looked eager.

'Not exactly,' said Nell, though it had been a sort of S.O.S., she realized. A call for help. Yet whether it was meant for her or had reached her accidentally, she couldn't tell.

TWO
Zed's Command

'Come on,' Menna yanked her arm. 'I can only hear the waves and even if there is a boat out there, we can't do anything about it.'

'People always say that,' Nell said in a puzzled way.

They spent a cheerful energetic hour playing with Marshall in the dunes and Nell tried to forget the strange message from the sea, tried not to listen for it, but it came all the same, every now and then, muddling her thoughts and slowing her down so that eventually Menna, exasperated by her lack of concentration, cried, 'You're hopeless, Nell. Even the dog plays better than you do.'

'I'm sorry,' Nell apologized. 'I can't help it.'

A deep whistle blew towards them and Menna yelled, 'I *can* hear that. It's Dad; he must be back,' and she tore away with Marshall yelping at her heels.

John Parry was a thin sandy man who stooped as though some bird of prey were perching on his back. His spectacles rested permanently on the end of his nose, revealing two kind myopic eyes, pale grey and ringed with long biscuit-coloured eyelashes.

'Hullo, Nell,' Mr Parry held out his hand while Nell searched his face for a trace of Menna's restless cheerful features, and found none.

'Hullo,' she said, taking the dry freckled fingers.

'Are you enjoying yourself?'

It was too soon to say but Nell politely muttered, 'Yes, thank you!' as they advanced towards the house.

'I've got some news for you both,' John said quietly, 'but we'll have to ring Leah before we make decisions.'

19

'Why? Are we going to do something dangerous?' Menna asked, hopefully.

'Could be,' John answered with a note of amusement. 'I've had a call from Mr Zed. He wants us on his island.'

'On the island,' Menna repeated wonderingly. 'But he's never done that. You told me he didn't like other people round him, especially children.'

'He's changed his tune, it seems,' said her father.

They had reached the peeled wooden door. Mr Parry closed it fast behind him, but too late to prevent the wind from hurling a fistful of sand across the floor.

'Have you told them?' Anne asked running for a broom.

'Yes, he has,' cried Menna, flinging herself on the worn-out sofa. 'But why has Mr Zed changed his tune, Dad?'

'Well, he needs me to discuss the accounts again,' her father told her, 'and he isn't entirely selfish, you know. He wants me to have my family with me because it's my holiday and he feels guilty for dragging me back to work.'

'Zed commands!' Anne said wryly. 'You're entitled to refuse, you know. You may be his accountant but you don't have to drop everything the moment he lifts his little finger.' She vigorously swept the sand into a pile.

'But you won't refuse, will you, Dad?' Menna pleaded.

'He won't want me,' Nell said quietly. 'I'd better go home.'

'Ah, yes, he does,' John replied turning to her quickly. 'He asked particularly.' He emphasised his last word peering at Nell as though she should know quite well that Mr Zed would want her on his island.

'Why?' asked Nell, wanting to go home. 'How did he know about me.'

'He knows everything,' Menna informed her. 'He's filthy rich and he has spies everywhere. He even does things illegally, doesn't he, Dad?'

20

'I never told you that,' John Parry said gravely.

'You've hinted at it,' Anne reminded him.

'Zed is very clever and the methods he uses to acquire land and property are ingenious, but it would be difficult to prove them unlawful. No one will ever know the truth about him, and I'm not sure that I want to.' John sank into a sagging chair with a sigh.

'I think I'd better go home,' Nell looked anxiously at Anne. 'They won't know where I am, if I go,' she turned to the window, 'overseas.'

'I'll give Leah a ring right now,' said John, immediately dragging himself out of the chair. It seemed almost as if Nell were the person Zed wanted, not his accountant.

'They won't want me to be so far away,' she insisted.

'But you must come,' cried Menna. 'Please be brave, Nell. I can't go without you. There's only Dylan and he's pathetic.'

How could she refuse to be brave. 'Maybe it will be all right,' she said, feeling breathless. And, all at once, she knew that the tugging voices across the sea had something to do with Mr Zed, whoever he was. And she had to find out what they were.

'We'll take good care of her,' Anne was speaking into the receiver of an ancient-looking telephone clamped to the wall. 'She and Menna are getting on just fine. Here she is!'

Nell took the receiver held out to her and answered Leah's cheery faraway questions. 'I'm OK. Yes, I'd like to go. Yes, it will be fun. And,' she added a little desperately, 'it won't be for long, will it?'

'No, darling,' came Leah's happy voice. 'You'll be having such a good time, the days will fly. You probably won't want to come home.'

'I will,' Nell said fervently.

Later, when the girls lay in bed discussing Zed and his island, Menna said, 'He's built a tower, Dad told me, that shines even at night. It drinks in the sunshine and the light lasts for weeks and weeks. It's made of crystal but you can't see into it, isn't that strange?'

'Perhaps it's too bright,' suggested Nell, 'and blinds you to everything inside.'

'I don't know about that. Dad says it's just one of its mysterious properties. They've got a generator on the island but Zed prefers candles to electricity. And they've got an old ship's radio for emergencies but Zed keeps it hidden.'

'Isn't there anyone else there?' Nell asked with a sinking feeling.

'Apart from his wife and son just these two people he rescued from prison. Dad says Zed likes to employ criminals. Ordinary people bore him.'

'But your father . . .'

'Good grief, no! He's not a criminal. He's just brilliant with figures and Zed offers a salary he can't afford to turn down. He has this ambition to be the most powerful man in the world does Zed, not just the richest. And his future is in the crystals. He's going to blast the ocean apart to find more . . .'

'He'll kill things,' Nell said in a fierce whisper.

'I suppose he will,' murmured Menna. 'I can't keep awake any more; I'm already dreaming of the way we're going to spend our holiday.'

'Who's Dylan?' Nell asked suddenly.

There was no reply.

'Menna,' Nell whispered urgently, 'who is Dylan?'

'Who?' groaned Menna. 'Dylan? He's Zed's son, of course. He's younger than we are. You'll hardly notice him. He never says a word and he's in the sea so long, he looks like water.'

'I think I know him,' Nell murmured. Why had she said that? She had never met anyone called Dylan, it was just the way Menna had described him that made him seem familiar: a boy who looked like water.

But Menna was either asleep or chose not to hear this strange pronouncement.

Nell tossed on the hard and unfamiliar mattress. The sheets crackled inhospitably and her pillow was lumpy and didn't seem to fit her head. Soon she would have to get used to another pillow and another bed. Perhaps on Zed's island, the light from his crystal tower would flood into her room and hold her awake for nights without end. This thought made her even more restless. She got out of bed and opened the window on to the balcony, glad of the winter pyjamas Leah had advised.

She was immediately soothed by the long rolling sound of the waves, closer now and visible in the moonlight. She folded her arms on the railing and gazed at the vast glittering ocean. She watched for that other light beyond the horizon and listened for its voice. But all she heard were real, familiar voices that drew her, almost unconsciously, along the balcony until she stood outside another window. From the room beyond she heard John Parry say, 'You're taking it too seriously.'

'Well, I'm concerned,' came Anne's soft voice. 'We're responsible for her. I don't understand why he was so insistent.'

'He wasn't insistent, love. He merely said bring the other girl. He meant her to be company for Menna.'

'But how did he know, John? How did he know about Nell?'

'I must have let it slip.'

'That's not true,' Anne said crossly. 'You admitted that you were surprised by his knowledge of our affairs. He's been spying on us. Why do I have this uncanny idea that it's Nell he wants and that we're just the bait?'

'That's absurd! Zed's not interested in children.'

'Who knows what Zed wants? I don't trust that man. You know I've never liked him. I wish you'd leave him, John!'

There was no reply. The wind tugged at the light curtains and Nell stepped away from the window, afraid that she had been seen against the moonlight. She thought she heard John murmur, 'I can't!' and then the conversation ended. Nell pressed her cold aching fingers to her cheeks and stood, breathlessly, waiting for more information. But there was only a sigh from Anne and a troubled rustling of bedcovers. Nell drifted back to her room and crept into bed.

At night Menna slept in the same carefree way that she rushed through the day; one arm flung out on the pillow, her head thrown back, eagerly prepared for her next adventure.

Nell curled into her habitual huddle, clasping her pillow like a life raft, closing her eyes tight against a light that no one else could see. For a long time she lay awake, her mind exploring a hundred strange reasons why Mr Zed should want her on his island, but never alighting on the truth.

THREE

A Room for Nell

They drove to the airfield early next morning. It was
very quiet and almost deserted; a private place that had
none of the uniformed activity Nell had expected. Not
even a coffee machine. And Zed's plane looked hardly
big enough for four. The pilot, dressed in jeans and a
sweater, seemed little more than a boy, but John
appeared to know him and gave Nell a reassuring smile
as he helped to strap her in.

'Have you flown before?' asked Menna as they left
the ground.

And Nell, gulping on an anxious message from her
stomach, answered, 'No!'

'It's great,' said Menna. 'I love flying! So does Mr
Zed. He flies everywhere, and whenever he wants Dad
on his island he sends his plane, WEEEOW – a giant
carrier-pigeon scooping up my father like a package.'

To Nell this description called to mind an illustration
in *The Arabian Nights*: the giant Roc with its talons
hooked in Sinbad's belt as it carried him off to feed its
huge, naked chick. She peered out of her window to see
a point of land vanish and an infinity of tumbling,
glittery water take its place.

Menna had packed her cassette player. Today she
wanted to talk. Stories of friends and enemies tumbled
out, getting lost in explanations, falling backwards in a
disorderly stream of unrelated incidents that left Nell
gasping. Who were these people that had bustled about
Menna's eventful life? How did she have time to learn
so much about so many?

Anne was already deep into the biography of a man

called Sam Higgins. There was a picture of a mountain on the cover. John frowned at columns of figures squeezed on to a sheet of paper resting on his lap-top computer. They both wore tinted reading glasses, like shutters drawn across the light. Nell had no way of knowing if they could hear their daughter's stories or were even aware that she was talking. Now and again Nell felt herself drifting away from the merry voice beside her and then losing the thread entirely. But Menna would tug her awake by demanding a response. Eventually, Nell found that a single syllable was all that was required. 'Yes,' 'No!' 'Mm' 'Wow' she muttered until Menna ran out of steam and allowed her to fall asleep.

When she woke up Menna was peering into her face, her cocoa-coloured eyes round with concern. 'Are you OK?' she asked. 'You were so fast, fast asleep.'

'Was I?' Nell muttered wearily.

'We're here!' Menna took Nell's hands and pulled her out of her seat. 'Come on,' she said impatiently. 'I want you to *see*!'

Menna's parents had left the plane but the pilot still sat in the cockpit, his tanned fingers tapping the controls, his head bent over the logbook. A shaft of hot light burst through the open door behind him and Nell found herself jumping down into a wide barren field. In the distance John and Anne were already following a blonde woman in a dress that was a mass of bright flowers. Nell, blinking against the sun, tried to balance in her new surroundings, tried to understand the hard, utterly unfamiliar pattern of glaring bleached rock and gaudy plants, but everything trembled in hazy unreality.

She passed a hand across her eyes and in an instant of clarity a boy swam into view, his white shorts and pale blond hair dazzling against the shadows behind him, his skin tanned so deep it almost disappeared. He stood unmoving beneath a tree with a mass of spear-shaped

26

leaves that sliced up the bright blue sky. Nell thought that he was looking at her but soon realized he was gazing over her head at something behind her, and while Menna plucked at her sleeve, she found herself twisting to look over her shoulder.

'This way,' said Menna releasing Nell. 'You're really what they call dreamy, aren't you?' She ran on, her pink arms flapping in the delicious sunlight.

Nell stood quite still watching the others vanish into a wall of stunted-looking trees. When they had gone she turned again and looked past the white blur of the plane, up and up, following the glittering skyward sweep of the crystal tower.

When she looked round the boy had gone, vanished into the foliage so swiftly she doubted he'd been there at all. She followed the thin trail of voices along a track studded with sharp stones, and wondered how a car would manage in such uncomfortable territory, remembering that, of course, they were on an island and didn't need transport.

The track began to wind downhill and Nell found that she was in a valley. Here the trees grew taller and the leaves darker. In their shadow the heat gave way a little.

A bird sang on a thin sad note and Nell stopped to search for it. But there was nothing to be seen. The leaves did not move at all. Running forward now, she glimpsed flashes of white through the trees and hurried on, a little anxiously, in case they had all vanished like the boy. The guiding voices had faded and the only sound in the world seemed to come from the unfamiliar bird.

At the edge of the trees the track ended abruptly and became a staircase of wide steps. And there they all were, looking up at her; Menna, Anne, John and the woman covered in flowers; a fuzzy crowd beside a pool that bounced dazzling lights at her.

'What d'you think, Nell?' someone asked in such a

27

respectful way it took a moment for Nell to recognize Menna's voice. 'Isn't it amazing?'

'Yes,' Nell said, looking over the glinting pool at the white building beyond. It was the most beautiful house she had ever seen, with shuttered windows opening on to balconies of flowers, a long wide verandah and fluted pillars ribboned with plants that climbed and swung in clouds of pink and ivory.

'Come on down,' said Menna gaining confidence. 'Delyth says we can swim. Beat you to the pool.'

Nell hovered on the steps. Where would they change? Did Menna know the house already? She stumbled down, fingering the clasp on her bag, wondering if the pool would allow a dark shabby swimsuit into its clear blue water.

Delyth led them round the pool, past tubs of red geraniums and up on to the verandah, while Anne muttered all the while, a little wistfully about how John had not prepared her, had never accurately described the house, and when they were in the wide tiled hall, hung with tapestries and furnished in dark mahogany, she seemed more flustered than before. 'Oh!' she sighed, and 'Ah, I never dreamed . . . John, you said it was just a summer house.'

'It is,' said Delyth turning on the curve of a wide marbled stair, 'and I sometimes wonder why I do all this,' she waved an arm at a gilt-framed mirror behind her, as though she had conjured up the richness reflected there. 'Few people see the place. No one drops by for chats and cups of coffee. There are no neighbours to call in the evening for cocktails, and Zed is always off somewhere. But when he comes back, sometimes without warning, I must have the house brimming with flowers and shining with polish, eternally ready for a party.' She caught her breath. 'Often there is no one with Zed at all but then he'll bring a foreign couple and their retinue. He calls them Joan and Freddy or Abdul and only when they've gone does he inform me that

28

I've been entertaining the Emir of – I don't know what, or Prince So-and-so.' She continued up the stairs, then paused and gazed back at her silent audience. 'But that's Zed,' she sighed possessively, 'so shut me up if I complain again.'

Anne gave a tight laugh. 'I should think we will,' she said. 'You live in paradise.'

Delyth turned away with a gratified smile, her delicate sandals trip-trapping up the marble steps, and Nell, following the procession of admirers, couldn't help thinking of Little Billy-Goat-Gruff, trip-trapping across the bridge while the big bad troll waited to eat him. Was there a troll in this house? Hiding in a chest or a tall cupboard? Because something was not right. Something unpeaceful rustled along the corridor that yawned away from the top of the staircase, something pattered at the heavy doors with their antique brass fittings, and shuffled away again as Delyth reached an open door and said, 'This is for Menna!'

Nell and Menna looked at each other, neither of them wanting to be the one who said, 'Aren't we together?'

Menna slid inside and flung her bag on the bed. 'Crazy,' she said and then seemed lost for words for, like Nell, she was probably reminded of rooms seen in glossy magazines or in heiress movies, where everything was large and dark and glowed with age and care, except for the pale silk curtains and the coverlet that looked like real lace.

My room won't be like this, Nell thought. My room will be small, with unwanted things pushed into it, and the sun won't reach through the window, because I'm an afterthought. She wished there was a frock in her red bag, so she could slip easily into the scene. In tee shirt and shorts she would stick out like a sore thumb.

They were moving on to the next room now, a replica of Menna's for Anne and John, but it was Menna who tried out the bed, inspected the wardrobe and exclaimed over the view.

'All the rooms face south,' Delyth explained. She didn't seem at all put out by Menna's tomboy admiration. 'And this one is for . . .' she hesitated.

'Nell,' Menna supplied.

Nell thought Delyth was about to call her 'the extra one'. She was embarrassed, perhaps, because the next room would be dingy and different and everyone would feel sorry for Nell.

But it wasn't like that at all. The third room was indeed different from the others, but not in the way Nell had expected. The bed was smaller and more beautiful, its tall headboard carved with flowers, its coverlet a pale rose – a girl's bed. And on the pillow, someone had placed a small golden-coloured bear. The tiled floor was strewn with bright rugs, there was a china doll sitting on a chest and a line of glass animals paraded across the dressing-table. It was not the tangible objects that welcomed, however, but more a feeling of thoughtfulness, as though someone had taken great care with the room.

'But . . .' Nell said, 'are you sure? I mean . . . is this someone else's room? A girl or . . . something . . .?' she finished lamely.

'It's yours,' Delyth said quickly.

'Thank you,' Nell murmured, glancing anxiously at the Parrys who wore puzzled smiles but were trying to look happy for her.

But Menna was openly envious and demanded, 'Why is her room like this? Mr Zed doesn't know her. It must be a mistake.'

'No mistake,' said Delyth with a cold smile. 'Zed's decision. It had nothing to do with me. Now if you'd all like to unpack, I'll meet you on the verandah for a drink. Tea? Or something cold?'

'Tea for me,' said Anne, and while John agreed, Menna piped up, 'Have you got a coke?'

'Zed's made sure of that,' Delyth said, 'and what would Nell like?'

Nell felt dissected, somehow. It was the first time Delyth had really looked at her and she seemed to be using the opportunity to gather in the details of Nell's face; her eyes, her nose and mouth were deeply scrutinized in a long grey stare.

'Just lemonade,' said Nell humbly. 'If that's all right.'

'Of course,' Delyth sailed away leaving a heavy fragance in her wake. A ghostly cloud of ungathered bits of colour moved into her path but Delyth walked right through it.

A little gasp escaped from Nell but no one seemed to notice.

'Well, isn't that considerate,' Anne said thoughtfully, 'to make Nell feel so at home without her family. You're a lucky girl, Nell.'

'Zed's full of surprises,' John murmured.

'Are you pleased, Nell?' his wife asked.

'Yes, very,' she replied, wishing they wouldn't peer at everything the room contained, like visitors at a museum. She felt guilty.

'I don't think it's fair,' Menna complained.

'Nor do I,' Nell said hastily and wanted to add that she was sorry, but the room beckoned and she found herself drawn in to touch the bear on her pillow.

'You wouldn't swap, would you?' Menna asked hopefully.

'That would be rude, Menna,' Anne said. 'Go and get unpacked.'

They left Nell to enjoy her good fortune. But Nell couldn't enjoy anything. She sat on the edge of her wonderful bed and worried. She hadn't wanted an inferior room but this would set her apart from Menna. And why had Mr Zed, whoever he was, done this? She knew from Delyth's resentful smile that she did not approve of these favours.

A mistake had been made! Nell was sure of it. Who was the girl Mr Zed really wanted, and what would he do when he discovered that shabby Nell had taken her place? He sounded an impatient sort of man; a man who could be very angry if he were thwarted.

Nell hung her head and noticed that a pair of white slippers had been placed beside the bed; they were decorated with tiny coloured beads and when Nell stepped into them she found they were a perfect fit.

She felt like the heroine in a new and dangerous version of Cinderella!

FOUR

Dylan and a Ghost

There was a new worry. How could she wear her rough dark clothes in a house of swishing skirts and tapping heels?

'Hullo!' came from the doorway. In the shadowy passage beyond Nell saw a pale blond head.

'Hullo!' she answered.

The boy stepped closer. 'Do you like your room?'

'Yes,' she said guardedly.

'My father's idea. I chose the bear, though. Did I do right?'

'Oh, yes,' Nell said, not knowing if she should congratulate him. 'Are you Dylan?'

'I'm Dylan,' he affirmed, padding into her room. He didn't look at all pathetic and Nell wondered if Menna had described the wrong person. His deep blue eyes slid thoughtfully about the room, finally alighting on her face. 'Who are you, anyway?' he asked.

'I'm related to the Parrys, in a roundabout way,' she explained. 'My stepfather is Mrs Parry's brother.'

'Oh!' Nell had the impression that her answer was not satisfactory. 'And because my brother is away for the entire summer, they all thought it would be a good thing for me to spend some time with Menna. She's an only child, you see. But I expect you knew that.'

'I'm an only child,' he said. 'Are you coming downstairs?'

'I've got a problem,' Nell said, wondering why she was confiding. 'I don't think I've brought the right things. I was expecting a beach holiday. I don't think I'll fit in here, your mother's so, well . . .'

'Bewitching, I know!'

'I wouldn't have said . . .' she began.

'Zed thought you might feel under privileged. He's seen to all that,' Dylan nodded at the chest of drawers. 'Look in there!' He slid away, without a sound, leaving no hint at all of the direction he had taken.

There were murmurs in the passage; the Parrys emerging. Nell ran to open a drawer. Inside there were layers of bright clothes, some still in their plastic wrappers. She pulled out each drawer, very fast, and left them hanging there, revealing their contents. Each one was filled with clothes for every occasion; bright, brand-new clothes with expensive labels, all in Nell's size. But if she wore them they would swallow her, disguise her; she would be printed with someone else's personality. I must hang on to me, she thought and tore herself away from the new wardrobe, just in time to follow the Parrys down the elegant stairs.

Menna, Nell noticed, had changed into an outfit that shouted sunshine and blue skies.

'Haven't you brought anything to wear?' Menna eyed Nell's crumpled tee shirt. 'This isn't a camp-site.'

Stung, but needing a friend, Nell replied. 'No. I wasn't sure, you see. You said we wouldn't be going anywhere.'

'I didn't know, did I?' Menna shrugged.

'I like that,' Nell nodded at Menna's skirt, feeling ashamed of her ingratiating smile. But it was worth it. Menna's face shone with pleasure.

As they continued down the stairs an overpowering smell of fish assailed Nell, and a column of ash-like particles swept past her. She couldn't restrain a choke of disgust. 'That's awful,' she complained. 'Whatever is it?'

'What?' Menna looked genuinely perplexed.

'Can't you smell it?' Nell was amazed. 'Dead fish. I can hardly breathe. It's like someone threw a bundle of desiccated bits downstairs,' and she looked over her shoulder half-expecting to see someone with an empty bucket or a plastic bag at the very least.

'Have you gone crazy?' Menna looked cross. 'All I can smell is flowers.'

Nell followed her, feeling the victim of a clever joke.

Delyth was floating round the verandah dispensing drinks with the movements of a ballet-dancer; she kept glancing at Nell and, at last, as though she couldn't help herself, remarked, 'You look hot, Nell. If you've nothing else to wear, perhaps we can find something more appropriate.'

Why didn't she refer directly to the clothes packed into the dressing-table, Nell wondered? 'There are some clothes in my room. Dylan said they were for me, but I wasn't sure. You couldn't know my size and they all look . . .'

'What things?' Delyth stiffened.

'Brand-new . . . frocks . . . and things,' Nell said timidly, afraid of the edginess that had crept into Delyth's flawless face.

'How wonderful,' said Anne handing Nell a tall glass of lemonade. 'You're spoiling Nell.'

'I didn't know about the clothes,' declared Delyth. 'If Dylan says they are for you, Nell, then Zed must have bought them. He is forever forgetting to let me know things. He only shares secrets with his son.'

An awkward silence followed the sentences that had tumbled fast and rather painfully from Delyth's perfectly-coloured mouth and then Menna remarked, 'Just the right size! It's amazing. Like a thriller.'

'Zed assumed Nell was your age,' Delyth smiled curtly. 'It was just luck, I suppose.' Then quickly changing the subject she asked, 'Would anyone like to see the beach?'

Everyone said, 'Yes!' 'Delightful!' 'Just the thing!' except for Nell who couldn't speak because the fishy smell was smothering her again, and a bundle of disconnected bits of rubbish was bouncing down the

35

verandah steps. She could almost make out a hazy shape against the pool and the trees beyond.

'Why don't you change, Nell?' came Delyth's distant voice. 'Try on some of those brand-new, just-your-size clothes.'

Nell could only concentrate on the hovering bundle that was slowly and unbelievably defining itself.

'D'you want me to come and help you choose?' asked Menna eagerly.

The little bits of blue and green background, breaking through the mysterious shape, began to disappear until they were blocked out completely by a very solid figure; an oldish sort of man in a thick grey sweater and corduroy trousers tucked into black wellingtons. He had a swirl of white-blond hair and his eyes were so blue it was like looking clear through his head to the sky.

'Well . . .?' Menna jogged Nell's arm.

'I . . .'

All at once the unlikely person gave a loud and very chesty cough.

No one seemed to hear him.

'I . . .' Nell tried again, gazing fiercely at the stranger.

'What are you staring at?' Menna looked towards the pool.

Nell took a deep breath. Her heart began to pound uncomfortably. 'That man,' she nodded in his direction.

'Oh, go and choose clothes by yourself,' Menna exclaimed in disgust.

Everyone looked at Nell, who obediently turned away. Bubbling lemonade from her tilted glass trickled over her fingers. She decided to leave the drink where it could do no harm and set it on a table. As she ran into the house she could feel sky-blue eyes following her through the cool spaciousness, even up the echoey stairs, and when she reached her room they disturbed her sight, like an after-image, when you have stared too long at something bright.

Nell closed her eyes, trying to blink away the unlikely vision, but she couldn't. Two bright blue halos forced their way into the dark behind her shuttered lids, making her cry out, 'Who are you?'

The lights disappeared and she opened her eyes to face drawers full of clothes, specially chosen by someone she had never met. This time she approached them cautiously, deciding to use just one item. The less she used, she reasoned, the less she would belong to this Mr Zed. If she wore just one dress for the whole holiday there was a chance she might escape him altogether. The part of her mind that was sensible and ordinary told the part that was susceptible to magic that this was silly and that no one was caught in spells these days. But as she drew out a sundress printed with rainbow-coloured birds, ordinariness began to slip out of her grasp. The brave attempt at a smile she had clamped to her face changed into a mischievous grin of satisfaction.

The dress was a perfect fit and Nell danced downstairs in bare feet to match her new tropical image. If she could have seen herself she would have been surprised to find a creature glowing with confidence and as dazzling and graceful as a dragonfly.

The verandah was deserted and the pool an unruffled sheet of turquoise, veined with sunlight. Nell stood beside the water and peered at her reflection. 'I don't even know where I am,' she told the floating version of herself.

'Zedland,' said a voice so surprisingly close she nearly toppled into the pool.

Dylan had sneaked up, barefoot, from nowhere. 'You look very good,' he said. 'Zed's clever, isn't he?'

'I still don't understand why I'm getting all this attention from your father,' Nell said. 'It can't be just to make me feel at home.'

'It can't,' agreed Dylan. 'But I'm as much in the dark as you are.'

37

This was disappointing. Delyth had given the impression that Dylan knew all his father's secrets. 'I was hoping you could, sort of, fill me in,' Nell said.

'Sorry.' His gazed flicked away from her to watch someone emerging between the shrubs beside the pool. The stranger in boots appeared. This time he raised his hand in greeting.

'Who is that?' Nell asked.

'Can you see him?' Dylan turned to her.

'Yes. It's odd, though. It took a while for me to find him all at once, as a complete person, if you can understand me. And your mother ignores him. She behaves as though he isn't there at all.'

'He isn't for her,' Dylan said wistfully.

'You mean she doesn't notice him?'

'She can't see him,' Dylan told her. 'No one can see him except Zed and me. It's really intriguing that you've spotted him too.'

'How can a person be seen and not seen?' Nell argued crossly. And she glared at the man who was now positively beaming at her. 'It's impossible. And why is he wearing all that wet weather gear in the middle of a hot summer?'

'It's all right,' Dylan said soothingly. 'He's my grandfather.'

A shock, like an icy hand laid against her cheek, told Nell that what she had been desperately refusing to believe was true. 'He's a ghost, isn't he?' she whispered.

'Of course he's a ghost,' said Dylan kindly.

FIVE

A Pillar of Stars

'You must be related to him, too. That's why you can see him,' Dylan was smiling broadly.

'I don't think so,' Nell said uncertainly. Though it did seem a solution to some of the mystery.

'There can't be any other explanation.' Dylan looked pleased to have found someone who could share his ghost. He must have been rather lonely, Nell thought, having to balance the two sides of his life; the company of a ghost with a mother for whom the ghost did not exist.

'Why is he here?' she asked. 'He seems a long way from home.'

Dylan didn't answer her directly. 'It does seem tough on him, doesn't it?' he agreed. 'But he doesn't feel the heat. He was a fisherman, that's why he's dressed for bad weather.'

'Oh, the smell of fish,' she murmured.

'It's bad isn't it?' Dylan sighed. 'But you get used to it.'

They watched the ghost gazing into the blue pool with a troubled expression, as though the colour bothered him.

'Have you told your mother about – him?' Nell asked.

'Yes, I did once, although Zed warned me it would be no use. He was sitting right beside me at the table and I said, "Mum, it's good to have Grandfather with us, isn't it?" But she just said, "Don't be ridiculous, Dylan!" And when I told her Zed could see him too, she got really angry. I suppose she felt excluded, as though we were playing a trick on her. She's jealous of everyone who gets close to Zed, especially me.'

'But you're hers. I mean you are her son, aren't you?' Nell asked anxiously.

'There's no doubt about that,' he told her. 'But being someone's child doesn't mean they have to like you.'

'Of course it does,' said Nell in a shocked voice. She could not imagine how it would be to have a mother who was not as kind as Leah.

'No,' Dylan disagreed, shaking his head in a matter-of-fact way.

The grandfather was approaching them, almost as though he wanted to join in the conversation.

'Can he hear us?' Nell asked.

'Oh, yes,' Dylan told her.

'And does he talk?' Nell had to know these things before she came face to face with a ghost.

Dylan considered while his grandfather drew closer. The fisherman had a gentle, lost expression and he walked with swinging, hesitating strides, as though he were not quite sure where his feet would land once they had left the ground.

'He talks,' Dylan said at last, 'but his accent is difficult to understand. He comes from an island in the North Atlantic. I think the sound of his own voice comforts him.'

'He must feel so alone,' Nell remarked. She was beginning to feel quite comfortable in the fisherman's unnatural presence.

'He does,' Dylan replied and he reached for his grandfather's hand. The old man smiled and seemed to touch the boy's fingers, but whether a real hand was pressed over Dylan's, Nell couldn't be sure. She withdrew a little, smiling uncertainly at the ghost, who returned the look with great warmth.

'She can see you, Grandfather. Isn't that good news?' Dylan said.

'Indeed! Indeed! I knew it,' he returned in a soft musical voice.

There was a shout from Menna somewhere behind them, and not wishing to be found in this odd situation Nell said quietly, 'I think I ought to go. I promised my friend, Menna . . .'

'We understand,' Dylan said gravely. He led his grandfather away as Menna came running towards them.

'You're another person in that dress,' she exclaimed. 'Let's have a look.' She swung Nell's arms away to get a better view, then leapt right round her murmuring approval. 'It's done something to your personality,' she observed. 'You seem much more – definite.'

Nell felt more definite. She felt dashing and slightly reckless and she wondered how the unknown Zed had managed to achieve this change in her with something as ordinary as a sundress. How had he guessed that there was a secret brightness hidden in a girl he'd never seen?

'What was Dylan saying?' Menna inquired. 'It usually takes him ages to talk to anyone.'

'He didn't say much,' Nell told her, not knowing how to explain a ghostly grandfather.

'He's pathetic,' Menna said scornfully.

'Why d'you say that?' Nell asked. 'He seems quite ordinary to me.'

'Perhaps he's changed for the better,' Menna said airily. 'It was years ago, well, maybe three, when I last saw him. Zed brought him to our beach house. Talk about a crybaby. He clung to his mother's skirt and wouldn't let her out of his sight. Anyone would have thought she was going to abandon him.'

'He was only a little boy,' Nell reasoned. 'He seems quite grown up now.'

'I'll give him a second chance,' said Menna, 'to please you. But he still seems weird to me,' and she glanced at Dylan's retreating figure, his fingers curled mysteriously round emptiness, his head inclined a little towards a grandfather she couldn't see.

Nell was tempted to explain. She was caught between two worlds and wanted, desperately, to keep a foot in both. But Menna was such an earthy person she would surely laugh a ghost away, or shut him out altogether.

'Come on! I want to show you the beach. It's amazing.' Menna was already leaping away through the trees and Nell felt she had no option but to follow. In the distance a plane took off; it flew low over the island and disappeared into a band of cloud. Nell felt truly abandoned. She tried to find a comforting memory of her brother, but only a fleeting, farewell picture came, of Ned setting off to meet their father, a huge rucksack slung across his back, noisy with tin mugs, penknives and water bottles. Ned was old enough, now, to sail with their father, but Nell would have to wait another three years.

She clung to her picture of Ned hoping the footsteps would come as well. But something got in the way. Shadowy fingers tore her smiling brother into ribbons, and instead of gentle footsteps, she felt the dull clanking of Ned's heavy rucksack, tumbling through her head.

'You are a dawdler,' came Menna's plaintive voice.

Nell ran to catch up with her. Desperate to escape the shadowy fingers that had sneaked into her mind.

They found Delyth and Anne lounging in padded chairs beside the sea, while John paced a strip of sand that dwindled into a blue and golden nowhere. Anne had adapted very happily into this new life of comfort, but her husband hadn't quite got the hang of it, Nell thought.

'We should have brought a game or two,' John called to Menna. 'Did you pack a ball?'

Menna shook her head. 'Perhaps Dylan has one,' she said, and running between the two women, asked, 'Has he, Delyth? A football would do.'

'I doubt it,' Delyth replied. 'I don't think he's that sort of boy.'

'What sort?' Menna probed. 'Every boy I know plays football.'

'Not Dylan,' Delyth said wearily.

'Doesn't he do anything?' Menna inquired.

'Not that I know of.' Beautiful Delyth closed her eyes, dismissing her son like someone she hardly knew, and a growing dislike prodded Nell into saying, 'Isn't he related, then?'

Delyth's eyes flew open and held Nell in a long frightened stare. No one else knew what to say. Even Menna looked at Nell in dumbfounded silence, and Nell, herself, felt all at once as though she'd been squeezed out of the Nell she knew, and pushed into another self. But as she found herself slipping back into the quiet person she recognized, she caught at a fold in her bold new dress, wondering if it was responsible for the accusing words.

'Of course he's related,' Delyth said at last. 'What a funny girl.' She gave Nell a look that was not in the least forgiving.

The older Parrys, hoping the uncomfortable incident had been overcome, both began to talk at once and Delyth entered the conversation almost too readily.

Nell and Menna raced away from the uneasy words. They skipped along the edge of the sea until the others were out of sight, then they ran on, not talking but laughing at nothing and kicking sheets of water at each other until they found themselves in a wide deep bay, cut off from further beaches by a high wall of rock that reached into the sea like a giant's foot.

At the very tip of the rock a boy perched like a sprite above the sea. He was so close to the edge that both girls knew at once what he was about to do. But before they could even speak the sprite took flight. He curved into the air like a bird then swooped down through the deep water with hardly a sound. Seconds later he emerged, far out in the sea, where he seemed to be striking boldly towards the horizon.

43

Nell and Menna watched without a word, until Menna said, 'I never saw anyone swim like that. Can it really be Dylan?'

'There's no one else here who looks like him,' Nell said confidently. 'He's not so pathetic!'

'No,' Menna agreed. She gazed thoughtfully at the empty sea. 'Why didn't his mother say? I'd be more proud of doing that than scoring a hundred goals.'

'Perhaps she doesn't know,' Nell suggested.

This seemed an extraordinary explanation and yet why would a mother not mention such a talent? 'He must have won prizes,' Menna said with puzzled vehemence. 'I mean it's Olympic stuff.'

'I don't think they have a normal relationship,' Nell murmured.

'I know what you mean,' said Menna. Dylan's extraordinary talent had brought her closer somehow. Perhaps the three of them could be friends after all.

They climbed the giant wall of rock and danced on the top like circus performers until they suddenly found themselves gazing at a sharp needle of light on the other side of the island, blazing into two shades of blue, like the legendary sword of Excalibur.

'I don't think I like that tower,' said Menna frowning at Zed's sparkling crystals. 'There's something not right about it; I mean not good, somehow.'

'Not good means bad,' Nell remarked.

'He's in there, dreaming up some plot,' guessed Menna.

'Mr Zed? What's he really like?'

Menna turned a serious face to Nell. 'Masterful,' she said. 'He wears strange clothes and sometimes jewellery. He's very tall and looks like a hawk. But he limps. He tries not to show it, but one of his legs is definitely wrong.'

Menna might have been describing an enchanter, Nell thought. She wondered why she couldn't hear the voices now that she was so much nearer to the tower.

Had she been wrong about them? They began at dusk, she remembered. She would have to wait and see.

That evening they had a candlelit supper in a long room whose walls were covered with portraits of other people's ancestors.

'Who is she?' Nell ventured, returning the gaze of a very plain lady in black lace.

'A Spanish Countess, I suppose,' Delyth replied. 'Zed acquired the paintings on his travels. He felt the need of a family. His disappeared so he invented one.'

This sounded interesting. 'Disappeared?' Nell repeated. 'All at once?'

Menna added, 'And all together?'

'Heavens no!' Delyth gave a real laugh. 'I didn't mean in a magical way, as in a clap of thunder or any of that nonsense. His parents died of natural causes and his brother and sister in unhappy accidents. He still has one sister, I believe, but to tell the truth I know very little about Zed's history. When we met he told me I must accept him without a past, and, of course, I did.' Glancing at John she added, 'Zed has a way of getting you to do exactly what he wants, while cleverly making you think it was all your own idea.'

'It's true,' John agreed. 'He's a bit of a magician.'

Opposite Nell, Dylan sat listening to the conversation with hardly any expression. There wasn't a glimmer of the extraordinary boy who had leapt into the sea. He had not said a word throughout the meal and remained a lost-looking creature with nothing to say for himself, until something began to happen to Nell.

At first she thought strange insects had been trapped in a lantern hanging above the table. She stared at it and found Dylan grinning at her. The sounds were very faint, not in a distant way, but more like whispers rustling near her head. Instinctively she put her hands up to protect her hair and Dylan's grin grew into a giggle of delight.

The adults glanced at him and Delyth said crisply, 'Is

that your only contribution to the conversation, Dylan? You might let us in on the joke.'

'Nell has heard a ghost? Haven't you, Nell?' His face was alive with mischief.

Nell was dumbfounded. How could she explain? Menna was glaring at her, sensing a conspiracy. Angry with Dylan for putting her in such an impossible position Nell decided to teach him a lesson. 'Ghosts don't exist,' she said scornfully.

The whispers retreated as though she had wished them away.

Dylan chewed his lip and avoided Nell's challenging stare. He seemed crushed by her remark and she wished she had not been quite so fierce.

Menna started yawning over her fruit salad and, as soon as the meal was over, she kissed her parents and drifted off to bed. Her bounciness had worn quite thin.

Nell decided to follow Menna's example. She offered to clear the table before she went to bed. But she was waved away.

'Someone will do it,' Delyth said airily.

Nell thought of the criminals and wondered where they were hidden. Avoiding Dylan's slumped, forlorn figure, she bid everyone goodnight and wandered off to bed. She knew she wouldn't sleep but felt that if she was alone she might be able to make sense of the whispers. Perhaps they would even come back and explain themselves.

She found a white nightdress among the clothes that had been bought for her. It had a high frilled collar and the sleeves and hem were edged with lace. Nell, who had always preferred to sleep in pyjamas, plunged delightedly into the old-fashioned garment. She found herself slipping several steps further into her new identity, almost as if invisible arms were tightening round her, holding her from tumbling back into the old uncertain Nell.

She admired the new girl in the long oval mirror. She

46

was pretty in a determined way, and the smile that had been planted so desperately on to her thin face, now seemed to flower there quite naturally.

Nell turned out her light and, expecting darkness, was surprised to find herself in a narrow path of brilliant light that fell through the half-open shutters. She ran to the window to look for the moon but saw only a pillar of stars shooting into the dark.

At night the tower was more beautiful than she could have imagined. Its strange light bathed the island and the sea in unbelievable tones of white and silver; true starlight. Or was it a trick of Mr Zed's? Was he an enchanter? Or an inventor who had threaded his crystal tower with energy from a secret source that he had tapped, deep within the ocean?

There was no doubt now that the strange voices belonged to the tower. It was as though every crystal had a separate voice, and every voice was whispering a message to her. But it made no sense. Nell was frightened and enchanted all at the same time.

She closed the shutters tight against the light but the voices still tried to find her, they babbled silkily against her cheek and through her hair. Later, when the house was as silent as a house can be when everyone is fast asleep, the tuneful whispers dragged Nell out of bed again.

She slipped downstairs and on to the verandah, calling softly, 'Don't you ever sleep?'

The tower winked and rustled until she had no choice but to go closer.

Feeling like the princess in the story of the golden ball, Nell followed her thread of light along the track that led through crowds of dense and fragrant bushes. She felt curiously unafraid of the night and the strange landscape because, she reasoned, there could be no villians, thieves or monsters on an island so small you could see one end from the other. 'I am alone and safe,' she told herself confidently.

But she was mistaken. Something was coming along the path towards her. By its drifting and undetermined motion she knew it to be Dylan's grandfather.

She had forgotten the ghost, and while she had been perfectly willing to believe him gentle and harmless by day, the darkness that surrounded the glowing and unreal path gave him a dangerous look. Ghosts belonged to the night. Wasn't it possible, therefore, that they might choose to be unkind once they felt more at home?

Nell pressed herself into the bank of shrubs but found that she dared not hide any deeper. A flurry in the undergrowth might frighten the grandfather into violence. If ghosts could be violent. She closed her eyes and froze against the leaves, her fists tight, her head averted from the light. A soundless breeze brushed her face then receded, like a wave. Nell breathed again and opened her eyes to see the ghost's square and somewhat mournful back hunching away from her.

He didn't see me, thought Nell, one bare foot stepping out on to the path.

'He saw you all right,' said a deep voice behind her, 'but he's a gentle soul and didn't want to alarm you.'

Nell's cry caught in her throat. She wondered if you could choke on fear and die, for she felt as though she might never breathe again.

'Did I startle you?' The voice was closer but it seemed far above her head and in a dreadful way it was familiar, though it brought no memories, only a cold feeling of dismay.

Slowly Nell turned her head and saw a tall man standing against the light. She couldn't make out any of his features for it was her face that bore the dazzling glare from the crystal tower.

'We meet at last then, Rainbow!' said the dark faceless man.

Nell's fear wrapped itself so tightly around her heart she could feel its frantic drumming in her head. No one

48

knew that her true name was Rainbow. No one in the whole wide world but her family. And this shadow was not a part of her family. Never had been. Never would be if she could help it.

How did he know her name?

SIX

Crystal Voices

'Come now!' The stranger laid a hand on her shoulder. 'Rainbows are never afraid. They can fly into the eye of a storm, bright as a jewel. I love rainbows.'

Nell twisted under the cool hand, trying to see the man's face, but he remained a shadow against the glittering tower.

'You came to see my tower,' he told her.

'Yes,' she agreed in a whisper, realizing that she had met Mr Zed at last.

'Come closer. I'm a proud man and I like to show off my creation.' He turned away from her and began to walk down the path of light that was filled now with tiny shining insects. And Nell found herself following, her eyes fixed on the tall figure before her, gradually learning its outline, which was broad and very powerful, yet somehow not so threatening now. There was something unsure about his long strides and she realized that he placed one foot hastily and lightly on the ground. In storybooks limping men were nearly always villains.

They walked across the wide strip of grass where the plane had landed, Nell keeping in the tall man's shadow. Not once did he look back to see if she was following. Here, where real moonlight reached them, she could see that Mr Zed's hair was very black and that he wore a frosty blue jacket, silky smooth, with tiny gems in the cuffs that glinted as he moved. It crossed Nell's mind that, in her sleep, she had stepped on to an island with no name and it was a dream that led her in the limping footsteps of a man who looked like an enchanter. If she turned in her bed she might step out of the dream and wake up.

But as they drew near to the tower she had to blink against its sparkle; the whispering began again and she knew that it wasn't a dream. The tall lame stranger was as real as the crystals that burned with their own secret light.

When he was within a few metres of the tower, Mr Zed stopped and, still without looking at Nell, caught her hand and drew her close beside him.

'What do you think of my pillar of stars?' he asked her.

'Think?' she uttered softly, surprised that he had used her description of the tower. 'Yes, they do look like stars.'

'Do you want to know what they are?'

She looked into his face for the first time and felt, again, that uneasy jolt of recognition. He had very strong features; an eagle's beak of a nose, a thrusting chin and eyes so shiny black they showed Nell only herself and told nothing of the soul behind them, unless it was to remind her of someone far away and best forgotten.

She glanced away to where the crystals danced. Some were only stones, she realized; they did not sparkle but presented a flat colourless surface to the world, merely glimmering with reflections from those that held the secret light. She stepped closer to the tower, taking her companion with her. Now she could see tiny stones, set like jewels between the crystals, and shells as smooth as pearls, some of them replicas of the shells that were strung on her necklace – shells from the furthest ocean.

'Where did you find them?' she asked, stretching her fingers towards the shells.

'That's my secret,' he told her.

'But I've seen them before, you see, those tiny shells.' She wasn't going to tell him where.

'Ah, yes,' he said, and now his mysterious smile

51

turned him into a true enchanter.

She reached again to touch the tower, stepping away from him too quickly for the warning.

'Not yet . . .' he began, but she was already reeling from the contact.

'It cried,' Nell accused him, staring at her hands in horrified astonishment.

'You can hear it?' Mr Zed asked calmly.

'There's something trapped in there and it's hurt,' she cried. Tendrils of sound were still curling into her fingers, threading their way into her head.

'It's just as I hoped,' Mr Zed said thoughtfully. 'Rainbow, you are a delight. We shall achieve something, you and I.'

'You must let them go,' she insisted, staring at her fingers while the little echoing voices ran through her. 'Can't you hear them?'

'I try,' he replied. 'And with your help I will be successful.'

'But who are they?' she demanded.

He brought his dark face close to hers and answered, 'Can't you guess?'

Suddenly, Nell didn't want to know who or what was locked into the tower with a hundred tearful voices singing at her. 'No,' she mumbled, and tore away from Mr Zed, slipping down the rock and flying across the wide field, never stopping until she reached the tangle of leaves on the far side. Now she risked a look back at the tower and saw Mr Zed etched against its sparkle. It was impossible to tell if he was watching her or his pillar of stars, for he was only a tall figure, as still as a waiting hawk.

Beside the pool, Dylan's grandfather sat in a wicker chair. He was gazing at the water and murmuring to it. A breeze ruffled the surface of the pool and Nell wrapped herself in her arms as she ran towards the house. The old man's mutter slowed her down and when she reached the verandah she stopped, in spite of herself, trying to make sense of his mumbling. She only learned, however, that the soft, sad pitch of his voice had something in common with the crystals, and this sent her scrambling into the house.

She took the voices with her; her fingers tingled with them. They were in her head, nestling there, like tiny birds, and she wondered if, in time, they would become a comfort to her, like the footsteps of the ocean that moved through her mind bringing her father closer.

There was a tap on the door. Nell had no time to answer before Dylan appeared. He was carrying a candle in a small glass lantern.

'I didn't say "yes",' Nell told him haughtily.

'Well, you'd hardly be dancing around outside of your clothes at this hour,' he replied with great self-assurance.

'I might sleep without anything on,' she said, finding the ordinariness of their conversation a relief after such an extraordinary evening. 'Some people do.'

'Not you,' he observed, setting the lantern on the floor. 'A lantern is very romantic, isn't it?' He perched on her bed.

Nell didn't feel at all romantic. 'I'm tired,' she said.

'I know. You've had a busy night. I saw you flitting about down there.'

He seemed to have forgiven her for denying his ghost. But why had he been spying on her? She didn't know how to explain her night-time excursion and settled wordlessly beside him, glancing surreptitiously at his earnest face. His features, sharpened by the yellow flicker of the lantern, did not seem entirely unfamiliar to her.

'I went to see the tower,' Nell said and added hesitantly, 'and met your father.'

'Roaming the island in his wizard's cloak?' said Dylan.

'You knew he was here? I thought he was across the sea somewhere and so did everyone else. Why didn't he come to meet us?' She felt affronted on behalf of her semi-relations.

'He met *you*, didn't he? That's all he wanted,' Dylan told her. 'Zed never does anything he doesn't want to do. He finds John Parry boring and describes his wife as a games mistress with an inexhaustible fund of childhood reminiscences, delivered in the most wearisome voice it's ever been his misfortune to experience.'

He had repeated his father's condemning sentences with such confident precision he had to be telling the truth. Nell was furious. John and Anne were kind people who did not deserve such cruel descriptions.

'Why did he ask them here, then?' she said angrily.

'Because they had you. And you were what he wanted.'

'Why?' she asked nervously. 'A week ago he didn't know I existed.'

'He did,' Dylan said emphatically. 'He's known about you for a long time. He's talked about "those two" for years. He never gave you names so I came to think of you as "the two". Zed told me strange stories of "the two", like fairytales but always with the sea in them. As I got older "the two" grew into children who were real, and gradually I discovered that Zed hadn't made them up at all, but just the stories round them. And then, all at once, just last week, you walked right out of the story. It was when he said, "Rainbow's coming," I knew that he was telling me about one of "the two".'

'Rainbow?' Nell repeated in a bewildered voice. 'How could he be sure that I was coming before I, myself, knew?'

'It is your name, then?' Dylan gave her an admiring glance. 'His exact words were, "Rainbow is coming so we've got to be extra-wise, and if we're very clever we shall be able to keep her."'

'Oh!' Nell said hoarsely, alarmed at being kidnapped from a story.

54

'Not that I wanted to keep you,' he consoled. 'I preferred to think of you where you were. But Zed built his stories in such a cunning way that you had been swimming closer and closer all the time, until "plop" you came right out of the make-believe world. Zed pulled you out in a manner of speaking.'

'I've always been real,' she said loudly and firmly, as if to reassure herself that this was true.

'I know that now,' he said, almost as an apology.

'It doesn't make sense,' Nell shook her head. 'Why would he do all this?' She flung out her arms and glared down at the pale flowers of lace on the nightdress that had been chosen for her. 'Why should he want to keep me, and how did he know my true name? Only my family know the real me. Zed is nothing to me, he is . . .' She wondered how to choose the words that would accurately convey her feelings. 'He's further than a star to me,' she concluded.

'He's not, you know,' Dylan said humbly, 'And nor am I. We share something, Rainbow, don't you feel it? I don't know what it is, but I do know that I'm right.'

She looked at him again and he returned her gaze, waiting for recognition. 'When I am close to my brother and my father,' she confided, 'I can hear the ocean's footsteps. All I get from you is silence, but I can't say that you are completely strange to me.'

Her words seemed to comfort him no end. 'I'm glad that Zed brought you here, Rainbow,' he said happily.

The use of her secret name must have caused her an involuntary shiver for he said quickly, 'Don't be afraid of me. I'm a friend. I didn't choose Zed for a father. He chose us both, you'll discover. But I'm on your side, not his. I don't know why he brought you here, and I'm not really sure why he called up my grandfather's ghost, but you both have something to do with the tower . . .'

'Can you hear it?' Nell exclaimed.

'No,' he said. 'Does it have a voice?'

'But I was sure . . . What were you laughing at then?

55

I thought you could hear them, while we were eating our supper. They were whispering in my hair.'

'I didn't know,' he said defensively. 'My grandfather was behind you. I'm sorry I laughed. I didn't mean to tease you.'

'And I'm sorry for what I said,' she admitted.

For a moment they silently regarded the flame in the lantern and then Dylan said, 'I shouldn't go in the tower if I were you.'

'Why?'

He shrugged. 'Just a feeling. Of course, you might not be invited. I never have been. No one has, in fact!'

'Even the men who built it?'

'They don't count,' he said. 'They were a bit surprised by the light but they made a joke of it. They thought Zed was some kind of nutty inventor. Zed put the roof on by himself.'

'Does *he* hear its voice?'

'Not exactly, but I've noticed that when he's near the tower, his forehead wrinkles as though he's got a headache, and then he'll smile mysteriously, as though he's fighting something, and winning.'

'They're very light, like tiny creatures,' Nell said sleepily, 'the voices, I mean. And they're sad. He's got to let them go.'

'I'm sure you're right,' Dylan said, looking straight at her with narrowed blue eyes. And then the boy, who was full of surprises, picked up the lantern and trod softly over to the door where he looked back, briefly, to mutter, 'Goodnight, Rainbow!' before vanishing into the soundless dark.

Nell crawled swiftly under the covers, pulling them over her head and closing her mind against whatever might be struggling to reach her through the Atlantic night.

She woke up to a warm breezy day, that greeted her with a joyful sparkle when she flung open the shutters.

The crystal tower looked feather-light. It might fly

away, she thought, if she so much as breathed into the air. The ocean was a glittery blue and the sky the same colour, above a ribbon of bright mist.

All the little ghostly voices had retreated and Nell found it hard to relive the scary and uncertain night.

Forgetting her resolution to wear just one garment from her new wardrobe, Nell found herself choosing red shorts and a white tee shirt decorated with bright abstract patterns. She pulled on the clothes without hesitation, pleased with the new determined Nell whose head emerged from a border of buttercup yellow.

Glancing into Menna's room on her way to the stairs, Nell saw that her friend had already left it. Clothes were strewn across the floor and the bedcovers were mounded in a heap beside the bed, as though they'd been responsible for a nightmare.

From the top of the stairs Nell could hear laughter and the clink of crockery. She was late for breakfast but found that, for the first time in her life, she was unconcerned about walking into a group of people she hardly knew.

Breakfast had been laid on a long table outside, and Nell ran straight into Mr Zed's unfathomable dark stare. He was sitting with his back to the pool in an impossibly white shirt that made him look less awesome than he had the night before. Anne, sitting next to him, said quickly, 'This is Nell,' and there appeared on his face a look of pleased surprise. 'Welcome, Nell,' he said. 'And how d'you like my island?'

Perhaps he was saving 'Rainbow' for less public meetings, she thought, and drawn into his game replied, 'I like your island very much.' If he didn't want anyone to know they had met, she wouldn't let him down.

A fleeting survey of the table told her that every place was occupied, but a second glance revealed a chair between Menna and John Parry that had possibilities. To most of the company it was certainly vacant for they all looked expectantly at the spare place. But Nell hesitated. For in the apparently empty seat, Dylan's grandfather sat gazing into a space above her head. He seemed to find her and smiled. There was something indefinite about him today, as though he had almost succeeded in wishing himself away. She was sure it was Zed's will that held him there.

Nell walked boldly round the table. Beside his father, Dylan watched her with interest. Nell stared back and withdrew the unoccupied chair with more force than was necessary; it flew out, and crashed back against the flagstones, but did not unseat the ghost. She carefully walked round the chair and drew it in behind her, while Zed's sly black eyes observed her with amusement.

Nell took a quick peep behind her, wanting to excuse herself for sitting on the ghost but had to make do with a silent apology. She hoped the grandfather would understand her predicament and disappear but when she sat down, although she could feel the edge of the chair, she had the sensation of sitting on something rough but very slightly ridged. A ghost's knee? The smell of fish was overpowering.

Dylan grinned at her with sympathy. 'Have some orange juice,' he said, pushing a jug across the table.

Nell poured herself a glass, wrinkling her nose against the smell of salt and herrings. She darted a reproachful look at Dylan, but he leant his head innocently to one side and she understood that, of course, if she had been down to breakfast earlier, she might have avoided his grandfather's chair, leaving it for someone who would have been happily unaware of sitting on a ghost.

The conversation that had flagged at Nell's appearance, broke out again. No longer the centre of attention, Nell seized her opportunity and pinched her nose.

'It's Dad's aftershave,' Menna whispered. 'It pongs doesn't it?'

'It does a bit,' Nell said gratefully, and wondered if anything could smell worse than fish. She was glad that Menna had decided to forgive her for her bright new clothes.

'I think he's trying to stun Delyth,' Menna said, rolling her eyes dramatically. 'But it's having the opposite effect.'

This was true. Delyth wore a closed look as John Parry relived, for her, his adventures as a teenage cyclist.

After breakfast the children helped Delyth to carry dirty crockery into the kitchen, which was very large and crammed with enough domestic appliances to fill three kitchens. The girls were surprised to find that the cook was not the round and merry person that cooks are supposed to be, but a tall gaunt man with fat-stained spectacles and a smudge of black bristles on his long chin.

'Pierre is a treasure,' Delyth told them, indicating the murky-looking person. 'I don't know what I'd do without him.'

This seemed very surprising coming from someone as scrupulously clean as Delyth. But criminals had hidden depths, Nell supposed. As she left the kitchen she was aware of Pierre's soulful grey eyes watching her and she had the uncomfortable feeling that he might be measuring her for something. She decided to visit the kitchen as seldom as possible.

On the verandah they were making plans. Everyone was going to the beach, except for John and Zed who were to discuss accounts. The grandfather had disappeared.

'I want to show you another beach,' Delyth explained. 'It's more difficult to reach but it's wild and beautiful. We might even glimpse a dolphin.'

Nell's heart leapt and Menna exclaimed, 'I'm going to fetch my camera.' All at once everyone had gone to gather what they needed for this expedition and, for a moment, Nell was left alone with Mr Zed. This daytime

Zed might almost have been ordinary, were it not for his glittery crest of hair and the eyes that made her feel like something's prey.

A woman suddenly appeared with a tray; she was very beautiful: an African with a long slender neck and silver hoops in her ears. 'Giselle, this is Rainbow,' Zed announced.

So now it was Rainbow again. Was Nell to live two lives?

The woman looked at Nell. 'Rainbow will do very nicely,' she predicted, placing Zed's breakfast cup and a coffee pot on her tray. 'Look at those clothes now, Mr Zed. Weren't they just made for her. Red surely is Rainbow's colour!' She swept away, all graceful curves and tossing hair, calling out, 'Bye now, Rainbow,' as she swayed up the verandah steps.

'I didn't know . . .' Nell began.

'Giselle is Pierre's wife,' Zed told her, enjoying her astonishment.

'Who is Rainbow?' Menna called from an upstairs window. A camera obscured the middle section of her face. Receiving no answer she shouted, 'Move closer to Mr Zed, Nell. I want to take a shot of the pool with you two in the foreground.'

Nell looked at Zed but didn't move. He left the table and came over to her. 'Come on, Nell. Oblige your friend!'

Nell felt a hand on her shoulder, drawing her close. Mr Zed's height blocked out the sun and smothered her. Her shoulder ached at the touch of his long fingers and she had the oddest sensation of sinking, and odder still of enjoying this sliding away from herself.

The camera clicked. They were locked in the camera now, Nell and Mr Zed. Together. For ever.

And then the ghost's anxious face came floating out through the gloom of the house.

He is afraid for me, Nell thought.

SEVEN

An Invitation to the Tower

'I need to get a swimming costume,' Nell mumbled.

As she broke free from the long fingers she heard Menna call, 'What d'you keep in your tower, Mr Zed?'

'A staircase,' he replied.

'Can I see inside, one day?'

'On no account,' Zed answered frostily. 'It's my sanctuary. Please keep away.'

So, now, Nell could never tell Menna about her privileged visit to the tower.

'He's weird, that Mr Zed,' Menna said as Nell passed her open door. 'You'd think he'd want to show off a place like that.'

Nell shrugged. 'You would,' she said. 'But perhaps it's not quite ready for visitors.'

'Don't be silly,' Menna said grumpily. 'He just wants to keep his old tower to himself.' An idea occurred to her. 'It could be that he's hiding someone there; a mad relative or a murderer who should have gone to gaol.'

Nell knew that whatever it was that resided in Zed's tower, it was not a shameful or a wicked thing. On the contrary, the sounds that she had felt were wise and very gentle.

'You look as though you'd seen a ghost,' Menna declared. '*Is* there something in Zed's tower? Has Dylan told you?'

'No . . .' Nell faltered. 'I don't know anything about it.' She hurried on, afraid of being tempted to tell about things she could never properly explain.

When everyone was ready Delyth led them, in single file, through dark foreign-scented shrubs that slapped their bare arms and scratched their legs. Someone had cut a very narrow path through the wood, without it their passage would have been impossible.

Nell began to enjoy the patterns of light on flowers that grew wild beside the path. She slowed down to try and identify them and walked straight into Dylan who had turned to find her. The others had disappeared completely.

'I know a quicker way,' he said. 'Want to come?' He looked slightly wicked, peering at her from under his heavy gold fringe.

'I don't know . . .' Nell said uneasily.

'Come on,' he urged. 'It's not dangerous and we'll be there ages before them.'

It was tempting. Nell couldn't even hear the others. If she lost Dylan she might be stuck in this leafy sea for hours. 'OK,' she said.

Dylan leapt away and a crowd of green shadows closed after him.

'Wait,' Nell called, plunging forward. She followed friendly and encouraging calls, pushing and stumbling until she felt dizzy with the sound of whirring leaves and the jostling of a hundred variations of green. She caught her foot in a snake-thin creeper and crashed into the flowers, lying there, stunned until she found her voice and cried, 'Wait.'

The encouraging sounds grew fainter.

'Wait,' Nell shouted from her flowery bed.

But Dylan never heard her.

She decided to be calm and sensible. Any direction, would eventually take her to sea or the house, so she rested a moment longer, examining a bruised knee and sore, greenstained hands. Something glimmered in the foliage, telling her that she was not alone.

'Who's there?' Nell asked nervously.

'You lost?' Giselle appeared, her hooped earrings glinting against the shiny dark hair. She looked almost a part of the tangled trees.

62

'I think I am,' Nell said.

Giselle extended her hand and pulled Nell to her feet. 'Best to come with me, little Rainbow,' she said.

Nell found herself bobbing through the trees, drawn on by warm silky fingers and knowing that she was not going to the beach, but to a place where Giselle had been told to take her. Soon she could feel the breath of the sea, and the wood was filled with a fierce, unnatural light. They emerged on to a sunlit cliff where the crystal tower swept up from its rocks to sting the air with brilliance.

'I knew we were coming here,' Nell muttered.

Giselle looked compassionate. She tenderly removed the scraps of leaves that clung to Nell's hair and clothes, as though she were tidying her for a party. 'Mr Zed wants to see you,' she said.

'Is he in the tower?'

'Where else?'

'But no one's allowed in there,' Nell said wildly.

'You are special, you know that, don't you?' Giselle stepped back to scrutinize Nell.

'Can you tell me why I'm special?' Nell begged.

'Sorry. He never tells us things. Zed saved us and we're grateful. We don't ask questions.' Giselle gave her a gracious, lazy smile. 'He said that your true name was Rainbow and that you belong to him.'

'Belong?' Nell said in dismay. 'But that's silly. It's a mistake.'

'I don't think so,' Giselle said calmly. 'Mr Zed will explain, I'm sure.'

'Where's the door?' asked Nell, hoping that this would pose a problem. She could see no sign of an entrance among the crystals.

But Giselle beckoned her to a faintly etched rectangle in the wall. Nell aproached it cautiously, then stopped in her tracks. The voices hadn't waited for dusk this time. They rustled expectantly.

Giselle took Nell's hand to lay it on a circle of shells

beside the door, and the voices stopped, like an indrawn breath, waiting for her touch.

Nell snatched her hand away. 'I don't want to. It's hurt,' she said, turning from the tower.

'What's hurt?' asked Giselle, who seemed to be truly puzzled.

'I don't know, do I?' Nell almost yelled. 'But I don't want to go in there, and I don't have to.'

'Of course you don't,' said a voice as the door swung inwards. 'But how can you turn away from your great good fortune?' Mr Zed stood in the open doorway, his white shirt now belted with silver, his wrist encircled with a golden chain.

A gust of voices streamed from behind him, catching in Nell's hair. They tugged at her fingers and stroked her arms and it was their insistence that took her into the tower.

Mr Zed held the door open with a satisfied smile, while Nell passed beneath his arm. She glanced helplessly at Giselle before the door parted them. The enchanter began to ascend a steep spiral staircase and Nell realized she had no option but to follow him.

His limp did not seem to impede him at all for he pulled himself upward, with surprisingly powerful arms. The voices became an ocean of words that soaked into Nell's skin like music, and she found she could almost translate them into a language that she knew. They were glad to see her but terribly distressed, and when Nell tumbled into the room at the top of the stair she had to kneel, exhausted on the floor, shaking her head free of the jumbled sounds.

They dropped to a mutter and then fell silent.

Mr Zed was regarding her with interest. He sat on a long white couch while, behind him, the sky swirled in unnatural shades and rosy clouds flew by, like wild horses.

'You can see something, can't you?' he said eagerly.

'Of course I can,' she said impatiently.

64

'What do you see?' He gazed at her, hungrily.

'I see the sky,' she told him, thinking he was playing a trick on her, 'and pink clouds like horses flying by. What am I supposed to see?'

'Rainbow,' he said passionately. 'You are wonderful.' He swept off the couch with no hint of a limp and faced what, to Nell, seemed to be a window, presenting her with his magnificent profile. 'I see only a wall of crystals,' he said ruefully. 'And I have an instinct that tells me the crystals have a voice, but I can't hear what they say. You can!' He whirled round to look at her.

'Why?' she spoke in such a small voice, she could hardly hear herself.

He dropped back on to the couch and pressed his hand to a cushion beside him. 'Come and sit next to me,' he said.

Nell got to her feet but perched lightly at the other end of the couch.

He smiled amiably. 'You will trust me, Rainbow, one day. And you'll want to stay with me forever.'

'I don't believe that,' she said resolutely. 'But I think you should tell me why you want me here. Why have you made so much fuss of me? It puts me in a very awkward position with my friend, but most of all, why can I see and hear the crystals in a way that no one else can?'

He was almost laughing at her now and seemed to have enjoyed her small outburst. 'Really, child,' he said. 'You must know the answer to the last of your questions. You are closer to your ancestors than anyone I know. You are almost pure, you see, and can hear things that our civilized, mongrel thoughts block out. You have kelpie's blood in you, and kelpies are born knowing the secrets of the sea. They are nurtured on the ways of the weather, they hear what the world has in store for us and in their memory they hold the secret of the universe, they know how it began.' The deadly blackness of his eyes stunned Nell, she waited

65

motionless, knowing what he was going to say next. 'I want that knowledge, Rainbow. And you can give it to me!'

In favouring her Mr Zed had released a girl of spirit. Where once Nell might have cowered, stupidly, she now said boldly, 'I'm not going to tell you a thing until I know where you found the crystals.'

For a fraction of a second, he lost his composure, but quickly regained it. He said easily, 'I raised them from the sea bed, thousands of miles from here. Dylan found them for me, I knew he would. I conceived him for the purpose.'

'How can you conceive someone for a purpose?' she asked, still feeling brave.

He laughed. 'I'll tell you how,' he said. 'I'm very proud of my success. A year before Dylan was born I began to feed my wife on fish and sea plant salad. I, myself, ate only food that had grown in the sea. Twice a day we bathed in the ocean, whatever the weather. I promised my wife that our child would be marvellous, unique and she agreed with the name I chose for him. We called him Dylan, after the magical boy in the Welsh legends, the golden-haired son of a magician, who leapt into the waves on the day he was born. I even chose Delyth for her Welsh forebears; she brought me closer to the child I wanted. I had to match my enemy, you see, with his kelpie children.'

Nell stiffened but she hid her surprise from the enchanter. Could there be another kelpie in the world, with children like her and Ned? Or was Mr Zed referring to Albie Nightingale. 'Your son might have been a girl,' she declared, 'then what would his name have been?'

Mr Zed smiled at the suggestion. 'He would not have been a girl,' he told her. 'How could he, when I had wished a legend on him.' He glanced quickly at her and then said regretfully, 'I have never had the daughter I wanted because Delyth grew sick after her son was born. She became a woman who couldn't have children. She even began to dislike the one she'd been given, I've been mother and father to him.' He looked appraisingly at Nell and went on, 'If I'd had the daughter I wanted, I would have called her Rainbow, for she would have been a prism of clear water with all the colours of the world leaping out of her. She would have been you, Rainbow McQueen.'

'I'm not Rainbow McQueen,' Nell said fiercely. 'I don't know how you found out about my first name, because only my family know it. But for all your cleverness you didn't go deep enough. My real name is Rainbow Nightingale.' Even before she had proudly spoken her second name, Nell realized that she had been tricked into telling the enchanter something that might put her in his power.

He was not surprised, however. 'I didn't think you'd take your true father's name after he'd abandoned you,' he said.

'He did not,' she cried. 'How did you know about my father?'

'Oh, I knew Albie Nightingale,' Zed told her, his voice growing steely. 'He gave me this,' and he tapped his lame left foot. 'I was the most agile boy on the islands until he chose to punish me.'

Nell couldn't hide her astonishment. 'You're from the islands?' she exclaimed. She thought she knew every family name from the place where she'd been born. Her Aunt Rhoda had recited them and Nell and Ned had repeated the names over and over. For every family there had been a story; the children had learnt their island's history through names, and Zed was not one of them.

'Zed is not my name,' said Mr Zed, reading her thoughts. 'My sister gave it to me when I was very small. I was forever muddling my d's and b's you see,

67

and she was such a clever one. "Zeb," she'd say, "you must learn to write your name correctly or the world won't know who you are."'

'Zeb?' Nell said.

His gaze slid cunningly away from her. 'To show my clever sister that I didn't care, I told the world my name was Zed. By the time I'd learnt my letters properly I found I'd grown into my new name and didn't want to part with it.'

'You must have a second name,' Nell said, 'everyone does!' Zeb meant something to her; it was a clue yet she needed another name to help her.

'Zed will do,' he said brusquely. He got up and paced about the blue room. Outside the window a cloud rolled by, like a gleaming whale, and in its light every detail of the man leapt out at her, every tiny crease in his face and in the luminous shirt he wore, and she was almost sorry that he couldn't see the colours he had built into his tower.

'Are you going to help me?' he asked.

And because she found that she wanted to please this hungry enchanter, Nell answered, 'What must I do?'

'Translate the crystals for me!' He sat beside her and captured the hand that held the distant voices. Opening her fingers, he said, 'Quartz has a memory. You knew that, didn't you, Rainbow? It grows beneath the earth in beds of volcanic rock. They mine it in vast quantities in Brazil and North America, but the richest bed of all lies under the sea. One day I saw Albie Nightingale's boat returning from the furthest ocean. I knew where he'd been because ice had cracked part of the hull and frost was melting on the rigging. When he came ashore he held something that glittered and he seemed to be listening to it. Later, he strung it on a necklace and gave it to my sister.'

'Your sister?'

'My youngest sister.' Something seemed to catch at him and hold him, for a moment, thoughtful and faraway. But, pulling himself back, he went on earnestly. 'Listen, Rainbow, I have made a fortune buying rights to gold and diamond mines, but it is nothing compared with what could be. I'll share it with you, if you help me. Long ago we lost that part of us that listens to our ancestors, but not the kelpie, and not you.'

She was about to answer him when voices behind her rustled like a warning, and she remembered their distress. 'If I do, you must take them back,' she said.

He released her hand and said icily, 'I am not mad,' and swinging into another mood he told her, 'You'd better go now. They'll be looking for you. But think about the crystals. Learn to talk to them and we can make a start.'

Nell found herself launched towards the staircase by the commanding black eyes, and descended the spiral while a distorted pattern of trees and flowers swam around her through the crystalline walls. The voices began to mutter at her again and dizzy with the effort of trying to understand them, she said crossly, 'Don't talk all at once. How can you expect me to hear you?'

Like naughty children the voices stopped abruptly and she was allowed to leave the tower in peace.

Outside, Nell stood blinking in the sunlight, trying to wake herself out of the strange conversation. But she couldn't shake off the feeling that she was caught in a net of Mr Zed's invention, and she would never escape unless she left the island. Almost without thinking she placed a hand against the tower to steady herself and a word sang into her fingers and travelled, clear as a bell into her head. 'Rainbow,' said the crystal.

And this time Nell didn't snatch her hand away but let it rest on the sparkling quartz and silently asked its name. The gentle reply that swam into her fingers was not a name. It was the memory of a creature with soft skin and a frill of gossamer round its neck, like silvery gills.

Nell's legs gave way. She tumbled on to the hard rock and heard her own bewildered voice cry out, 'I know who you are.' And then she was drifting on the ocean floor between bands of glowing fish.

EIGHT
Grandfather McQueen

'What happened?' Framed by a pale curtain of hair, Dylan's brown face peered down at her.

'I think I went to sleep,' Nell said.

'You'll get sunstroke,' he told her. 'Everyone's looking for you. Did you get lost?'

'Not exactly. Giselle brought me here to see your father.'

'That's odd.' He rubbed his head. 'She said she hadn't seen you.'

'She would, wouldn't she?' Nell said angrily. 'She'd do anything your father told her. He saved her, didn't he? From some terrible fate in the country where she comes from.'

'How d'you know that?' Dylan asked suspiciously.

'She told me.'

'Oh!' He looked concerned. 'Have you been into the tower?'

'I didn't have much choice,' she said.

'I warned you not to,' he reproved. 'What did you see?'

Nell got to her feet wearily listing the images that he would never see, 'Sky like the sea, clouds on fire, trees and plants in colours that don't exist any more and . . .' She couldn't tell him about the tiny creature that might have been the beginning of life on earth.

'Let's get away from here,' he said, and he ran into a forest of stunted trees that crept towards the rock.

Nell followed, down a path that fell sharply to a narrow beach. She found Dylan sitting with his back to a tall weed-covered rock and dropped down beside

71

him. They were silent, for a moment, watching the warm Atlantic steal over the sand and then Dylan said, 'My father only tells me half the truth.'

'He doesn't know it all,' she said, unconsciously defending the enchanter. 'I'm the only person who can see those things inside his tower.'

He looked at her, over the arms that hugged his knees. 'You're very odd,' he said.

'Your father told me that he fed your mother with fishes so that you'd be a great swimmer,' Nell said. 'He told me that they named you after the boy in Welsh Legends, who swam on the day he was born.'

'That's true,' he admitted.

'And is it true that you swam deeper than a pearl diver, to bring him the crystals from the furthest ocean?'

'Yes,' he nodded.

'You can't deny that's odd,' she said, and receiving no reply added, 'So we're both odd. Both irregular and curious human beings.'

'I suppose so.' He sighed.

Nell probed further, 'Zed told me that a man called Albie Nightingale made him lame. Why would he do that?'

'He was stealing eggs,' Dylan explained. 'Zed did things like that and isn't ashamed of them. He told me that a pair of birds came to the islands every spring. They were very rare, only five pairs in the whole of the North Atlantic. They laid their eggs on the cliffs, on thin ledges high above the rocks. No one could reach them. But my father decided to get just one egg for himself, I suppose he thought it would make him special in some way, to have something that was forbidden. They are a protected species, you see.'

'Go on,' she encouraged.

'Zed was a great climber, even Grandfather agrees with that, "Nimble as a lizard, my son," he says. He climbed in bare feet and with nothing to help him but a little pick, tied to his belt on a piece of string. The route down the cliff was a sheer drop so he swam round from the beach and began to climb up from the rocks.'

'How old was he?' Nell asked, trying to imagine the Zed she knew, swimming in a velvet coat with gems sewn on to it.

'Twelve,' said Dylan and, glancing at her, added, 'so was Albie Nightingale. He was a weird boy, my father said. No one knew where he came from. He was looked after by two old people, who had no children of their own, but their name was Dugan.'

'I know Albie Nightingale's past,' Nell said sharply. 'He's my father!'

'Your father,' Dylan said incredulously, 'but . . .'

Nell didn't give him time to explore this piece of information. 'Perhaps Zed saw my father's history in a crystal ball,' she said with desperation, 'and used this knowledge for some secret purpose. I don't believe they knew each other. Zed is not an island name, and nor is Zeb.'

'He hasn't invented his lame leg,' Dylan insisted, as though his father's limp could excuse both his name and his behaviour. 'All right, he can see the past, he can bring people back, he's practised it. He's an enchanter, if you like, but it's the truth about Albie Nightingale trying to kill him. And he's your father? I can hardly . . .'

'My father tried to kill him?' Nell said hotly. 'That can't be true.'

'Let me tell you,' Dylan said patiently. 'Zed was climbing this cliff, like I said. He could see bits of grass and feathers to show him where the nest was built, and he could hear the bird grunting, like a warning. But that didn't put him off. He got closer and closer and was just an arm's length away from the nest when something grabs his ankle like an iron fist and he looks down and sees Albie Nightingale. "Get down," says Albie. "Oh, no," says my father, "I've got this far and I'm going to get that egg." "I'll see you dead, first," says Albie. "No

73

you won't," says Zed and he kicks out trying to shake Albie off his foot, and probably off the cliff too. "Then you'll be killing my brother," says Albie, and he did a weird thing . . .'

'What?' asked Nell, lost in this story of her father.

'He made a noise, my father said. And the next thing my father knows, the bird above him shrieks out an answer and flies at Zed, her talons ready to tear out an eye, and at the same time he feels a great tug on his leg and down he goes. He fell on the rocks with one leg all crushed under him, broken in three places. They flew him to the mainland and although he had four operations they never did set the bone quite straight. But do you know,' Dylan said quickly before Nell could break in, 'my father never told a soul who did it, until he told me.'

'He was stealing eggs,' Nell commented. 'He couldn't tell.'

'In his whole life Zed has never been ashamed of anything. It wasn't that,' Dylan said gravely. 'When he was lying on the rocks with his leg all smashed and hurting too bad for crying, my father looked at the cliff and there was no one there.'

'No,' agreed Nell softly.

'Albie Nightingale had either climbed an impossible cliff or dropped on to the rocks below. But he was nowhere.'

Father and son must have discussed this riddle a hundred times, Nell thought. Dylan knew the story like a well-rehearsed nursery rhyme. He had conjured up the boy Zed as though it had been himself. And although she knew the answer to their riddle, she couldn't give it to him. Albie Nightingale had not been named Albatross for nothing. But Dylan wouldn't believe what she could tell him. Or had she misjudged him?

'What about the bird?' Nell asked cautiously.

'It joined another cloud of birds between my father

74

and the sun, and they all flew into the sea.'

'That's it then,' Nell said, not bothering to explain.

Dylan looked sideways at the ocean. If he believed what she was trying to tell him, he gave no sign of it. 'Albie Nightingale is the only person in the world my father is afraid of,' he said. 'But he admires him too, you know. He wants to meet him, just once more.'

It sounded ominous that 'just once more'. 'Why?' she asked.

'To see who will win!'

As he said this Dylan's blue eyes found something on the cliff behind them and Nell, turning to follow his gaze, saw a dark figure beside the glowing tower. Something watchful and predatory in Mr Zed's attitude alerted her and, all at once, she began to know who he was.

'He's glad we're together,' Dylan said, as though hoping to please her. 'He wants us to be friends so that you'll stay.'

'Zebedee!' Nell's voice shook.

'That used to be his name,' Dylan confirmed, puzzled by her distress.

Nell couldn't trust herself to say any more. Her Aunt Rhoda had taught her to be so frightened of that name that she'd tried to bury it under a mountain of happy memories. But now Zebedee had leapt out, without warning, right in front of her, and all she could do was try and hide from him.

'What is it?' Dylan asked. 'Don't look like that. There's something we ought to . . . I'm trying to work it out. Albie Nightingale married my father's sister, and that means . . .'

Nell sprang away from him. He was a part of Zebedee. His son. Part of the plot to catch her.

'Where are you going?' He looked hurt and angry but she couldn't help that. Turning away she fled towards the trees and ran until she could hardly breathe, hiding from everything, even the voices that had been stolen

75

out of the sea. But she couldn't hide from her aunt's warning, 'Zebedee should never be anyone's father. We were all a little afraid of him . . . He wanted you so badly he hounded his own brother until he drove off the cliff and you were nearly drowned.' Zebedee, the wicked boy who called up ghosts, imperious as a thunderstorm. Zebedee, the man who had driven Leah's first husband to his death.

Nell stayed in the trees for an hour or more, she lost track of time. When she finally emerged and walked on to the hot tiles beside the pool, her tears of distress had dried into a bright pattern on her cheeks.

'What is it?' Menna cried, scrambling out of the pool. 'What's frightened you, Nell?'

'I'll tell you later,' Nell said. She badly needed to share her grim discovery but would Menna listen to such an unlikely story? Would she even attempt to believe?

'Where have you been, Nell?' Anne ran out of the house, her plump arms pink from the sun.

'I got lost,' Nell said lamely, 'and . . .' She found that she couldn't even mention the tower and Zebedee.

The master of the house did not appear again that day, but Dylan wandered in for lunch, looking solemn. He didn't say a word to anyone and disappeared immediately after the meal was over.

'Tell me about it, now,' urged Menna, when Dylan had gone. 'Something funny's going on.'

But Nell wanted to wait until they were safe from interruptions. 'I'll come to your room tonight,' she said.

For supper Delyth wore a romantic white cloud of a dress. Nell could tell that she had chosen it to match her husband's outfit. They should begin the meal without Zed, his wife advised, because he was always late, and while they ate Delyth chattered and nodded like a bright bird, never glancing at her husband's empty chair, or at her wrist where a little silver watch could tell her that it was too late; that Zed was never coming.

76

He never came. Nell watched Delyth wilt behind fast talking and false laughter, and felt guilty somehow.

She couldn't meet Dylan's bewildered eyes; couldn't trust herself to look at her own true blood-cousin; she was afraid she would begin to relent a little. She must keep remembering he was Zebedee's creation, so she let her gaze wander across the antique portraits and the faces of her semi-relations, but never let it rest on Dylan. She was grateful for the Parrys' enthusiastic conversation. John knew about everything, it seemed: rocks and fish and weather patterns and it was almost possible to become so engrossed in his stories that she could ignore the empty chair and the silent boy beside it. But after a while the space where Zed should have been began to grow; it widened into a yawning void that called attention to itself in such a way that it might have been a giant chasm, and it dawned on Nell that Mr Zed had called up this watchful nothingness just to remind them all that they belonged to him. Nell, perhaps, more than anyone else. She tried to concentrate on John Parry's kind, freckled face, but his comments slipped away from her and once again she became aware of the looming high-backed chair that belonged to Mr Zed. It was no longer empty!

Dylan's grandfather had come to take Zebedee's place. He smiled at Nell and put one hand over his grandson's fingers. Dylan looked up at him gratefully, then turned to Nell. This time she couldn't avoid the doubled strength of their sky-blue eyes. A little gasp broke from her as she suddenly realized that she was looking at her own grandfather.

'What is it, Nell?' Dylan spoke into the surprised silence that followed Nell's exclamation.

'Nothing,' she said. 'I just feel sort of . . .' She couldn't think of a suitable ailment and so asked desperately, 'Could I go to bed?'

'Of course, dear. Would you like me to come up with you?' Anne offered.

'No!' Nell stood up, staring wildly at her grandfather. He looked anxious and, for a moment, she thought he might come over to her. 'It's nothing, really. I just want to lie down,' she said backing away from the table.

Menna swung round and said, 'Are you sure you're OK, Nell? You look peculiar!'

Nell grinned half-heartedly and reached the door. 'I'm OK,' she insisted. 'Goodnight, everyone, I'm sorry to be . . . so . . .' She turned into the hall and closed the door behind her.

Safe in her room Nell sat on her bed and picked up the small golden bear. 'I want to go home,' she told him. 'I don't want to be Rainbow, although it makes me feel good. I like the things he's chosen for me, that's the trouble. And that includes you. I should throw you through the window and tip his clothes into the sea. But I can't,' she tucked the bear carefully into bed, 'because he's an enchanter.'

Someone knocked on the door.

'Come in,' Nell said, hoping it would be Menna.

Delyth looked in. 'I want to talk to you,' she said. She wasn't that sharp little bird any more but all frayed, like a beautiful design that was breaking apart. She walked right over to the bed and sat beside Nell. 'I hope you don't mind,' she said.

'Oh, no,' Nell replied, intrigued but apprehensive.

'It's a lovely room, isn't it?' Delyth assumed a politely interested expression.

Nell said, 'Yes, I feel very lucky.'

'And Zed did it all for you. The clothes and everything.'

'Yes.'

'D'you know why?'

'I'm beginning to,' Nell said uneasily. 'I think he wants to keep me here.'

'And do you know why he wants to keep you?' Delyth couldn't disguise her hungry curiosity any more.

'Well . . .' Nell began, 'he's been trying to get me for a long time it seems.'

'I thought so!' Delyth brought her hands up to her face. She hunched her shoulders in a long and silent sob.

Dismayed and puzzled, Nell dared not move. She sat beside Delyth unable to touch or comfort her.

At length Delyth rubbed her wet face with ringed fingers, but she could do nothing about her red-rimmed desperate eyes. 'You're his, aren't you?' she said harshly.

'No!' Nell said indignantly. 'I like the things he's given me, I can't help it. Because with all these new clothes I'm brighter, and it makes me feel good, but I won't belong to him, ever. You can be sure of that. He can't keep me here.'

'If you're his child, he can,' Delyth said.

'I'm not his child.' Nell leapt off the bed, amazed and horrified at Delyth's conclusions.

'But I thought . . .' Delyth began to look uncertain, even hopeful. 'Then why all this?' She indicated the room and the embroidered shirt that Nell was wearing.

Nell sighed. 'I don't think I can ever begin to make other people understand.'

'You're positive that you're not Zed's daughter?'

'Of course, I'm not,' Nell exclaimed. 'I know very well who my father is. He's Albie Nightingale. There's no mistake about it.'

She could see that Delyth still doubted her, but there was nothing she could do. She couldn't prove that she heard the ocean's footsteps or that she felt the thoughts of creatures who had died. 'Please believe me,' Nell said. 'I know who I am. Zed is my uncle. I've only just found out.'

'Your uncle? Why didn't he tell me?' Delyth asked suspiciously. 'It's such a simple piece of information. Why wouldn't he tell me, to put my mind at rest, knowing what I thought?'

'Perhaps he didn't know,' Nell suggested, trying to

sound wise. 'Perhaps he never even imagined you would think I was his child. I don't know why he doesn't tell you things,' she said with sympathy. 'But he's a strange man, isn't he? The sort of man who needs to keep secrets, from what I've heard. I expect there are things about Zed that no one knows, not even Dylan.'

'I doubt that,' said Delyth, her composure returning. She stood up with a smile that tilted her mouth but never reached her eyes, and walked briskly across the room, then, turning suddenly, she asked, 'You're sure you're not his child? You can prove it?'

'Of course,' Nell said. 'I've got a birth certificate. My father could tell you, and my brother, if they were here. I wish you could meet them, they're so . . .' She hunted through her store of memories, looking for a way to describe Ned and Albie Nightingale, longing for the comfort of their voices and the rhythm of the ocean's footsteps, but once again, all she could find was Ned walking away from her, his face disappearing behind a fence of dark fingers and his rucksack rolling through her mind like dull thunder. And although she was very frightened by this she could see that beneath Delyth's cool grey stare, there was an aching sort of loneliness that was even worse than fear, and she felt compelled to help her.

'I promise I'm not Zed's child!' Nell put all the authority she could muster into her words. The effort was almost beyond her.

She was rewarded with a sigh and then a glimmer of a real smile before Delyth walked away. Nell could hear her hard little heels hitting the polished floor like the ticktocking of a slightly mad clock, and wondered if she'd helped at all.

'It's not my fault she's unhappy,' Nell said, cradling the golden-haired bear. For a moment she felt at odds with the new sort of girl she had become and wasn't sure that she enjoyed giving advice and sympathy to someone else's mother. She would have preferred it to have been the other way around.

She changed into the white nightgown and lay on the bed until every sound in the house had died away. Then she crept down the corridor to Menna's door, which stood ajar.

'Are you awake?' Nell whispered into the dark room.

Menna's deep sleep was evident in the slow and peaceful breathing Nell could hear; it was the only sign that Menna was there at all for nothing could be seen in the room; the only light came from the stairs at the end of the corridor. Too wide awake, now, to go back to bed, Nell was tempted towards the warm glow of the light. She reached the head of the stairwell and looked down.

The lamp was standing on an oak chest, its polished lid unable to disguise the scars of time and travel. As Nell gazed down on the ancient and rather comforting surface of the chest, a grey-clad arm appeared, as if from nowhere, and raised the lamp an inch or two. Illumined by lamplight, the ghost's face looked so warm and real Nell found it hard to believe that he was not flesh and blood but just a bewildered-looking image of himself. He was not an old man but his skin had been carved into ragged patterns by the weather. He was probably not much older than Zed, Nell thought.

The ghost must have sensed her presence for he looked up at her and called softly, 'I canna find it.'

'What are you looking for?' Nell whispered, approaching her grandfather down the wide staircase.

'I canna tell,' he looked wistfully at the oak chest. When Nell stood beside him, he said, 'Hold the lamp, there's a good lassie.'

Nell obediently took the lamp and with an intense and hopeful expression, he swung open the lid of the chest. It was empty. A look of terrible desolation passed across the fisherman's face.

'What is it?' Nell asked, stretching her free hand towards her grandfather. She imagined that she might

81

find only empty air but was surprised by an indefinable roughness under her fingers. It was not quite solid and yet she knew that she had made contact with something.

The ghost sadly shook his head. He closed the lid, took the lamp from Nell and set it carefully on the chest. 'I thought that maybe there'd be something there,' he said. 'It was mine, you see, that chest. It came from the old place.'

Nell stared at him uncomprehending.

'From home, lassie,' he explained. 'I kept my tackle in it and I hoped, maybe, there'd be something left – a bit of twine, maybe, or a hook . . . to lead me home.'

'Perhaps . . .' She hardly dared to suggest it, for it seemed such an undignified solution, but still – 'Perhaps, if you got in the chest it would . . . sort of . . . take you where you want to go.'

He looked at her gratefully but shook his head. 'I've tried it, lassie, but he's done something to it. He's made my chest his own, it will not budge.' His voice now boomed and gurgled rather like an underwater cavern and Nell hoped that no one in the house would be disturbed by such a fearful sound. 'He's brought me here, that wicked boy,' the ghost went on, wheezing dreadfully, 'and he will not let me go.'

'Why did Zebedee bring you here?' asked Nell in a whisper, hoping that the ghost might follow her example and at least lower his voice.

'He thinks I hold the secret, that evil son of mine,' the fisherman complained, obligingly softening his tone. 'He plunders the past and he should not. He wants too much, that boy.' It seemed that the ghost still thought of Zebedee as a wicked child. 'His mother spoiled him.'

At last Nell allowed herself to remember Grandmother McQueen, Zebedee's mother, who had hated her and Ned because they were the children of Albie Nightingale. And she began to understand her.

The ghost ambled soundlessly across the hall. He

stopped and beckoned to Nell who tiptoed to his side. Together they trod carefully over the marble tiles and on to the verandah. And, although their passage seemed silent, Nell could discern the heavy tread of damp boots, pressing into the stillness. A sound that was not a sound but an echo in her head, telling her about a fisherman, a listing boat and a vast and dangerous sea.

Outside, her grandfather lowered himself into a wicker chair, a seat that usually creaked in a disgruntled way but now gave no hint of any weight upon it.

'Your name is Alistair McQueen,' Nell said softly. 'And you are my grandfather.'

'Aye,' he replied without surprise.

'And Dylan's.'

'Aye.'

'It's sad that you never knew us,' she said, all at once finding a strange contentment in his company.

'I know you now, Rainbow Nightingale,' he said warmly. 'I can read your history. You are a true sea-child. Not like Dylan, who was engineered by his father's greed and curiosity.'

'My brother is the same as me,' Nell told him. 'But we don't really know what we are, only that we're a bit different from other people.' Suddenly she found herself adding in a breathless way, 'Our father's father was a kelpie.'

'Aye, I know what you are, lassie,' murmured the ghost. 'I knew Albie Nightingale. I learned more about kelpies than anyone, and I know about their treasure. That's why Zebedee has brought me back.'

Nell had always longed to know how and why a kelpie was. What made them different and how they first began. She had discussed it with Ned so many times, but never with anyone else. Their father's visits were such rare treats they spent every moment with him talking about the creatures he had saved at sea, reliving, with him, his days away from them. And somehow in their rushed and breathless happiness they had never had time to ask him more about their strange inheritance. The way Ned could draw the ocean round him, like a blanket, to keep out pain, the way Nell, herself, could hear the ocean's footsteps in her head. She had found, at last, the person who knew these things and might tell her without her even asking.

'It is my belief,' said Nell's grandfather, 'that once, long before we were what we are now, there were those who lived on land and those who lived in the sea and there was no great difference between them. But while the land-dwellers grew rapidly into creatures who needed to tease their minds with experiment and invention, those who remained in the ocean kept in touch with the earth's language and had no need to invent. They retreated from the land-dweller's greed and cruelty to the furthest ocean, beyond the islands where you and I were born, Rainbow; an ocean deeper than any other, closer to the heart of the world. No human has ever been there, nor ever will. They'll break through the universe and reach stars we haven't even seen, but they'll never find the secret in the furthest ocean.'

'But they have, Grandfather,' Nell said, looking at Zed's crystal tower. 'Your son took those crystals from the furthest ocean, he said he did.'

'Nonsense. They're but fragments, lassie. Caught on the edge. He never reached the greatest treasure.'

'What is the greatest treasure, then?'

'It's a valley of quartz, miles wide and deeper than anyone can tell. It keeps the light from a million years ago and it holds the mystery of how life began; every crystal can tell a part of that true and eternal story. Can you think of anything more precious, Rainbow?'

She could not, and silently shook her head.

'Once in a while,' her grandfather went on, 'a whaler records a sighting. He has seen a vast pool of light in an otherwise dark and stormy sea, and he has been

84

tempted nearer. But its power and beauty overwhelms even the most destructive of men, and they have always left it in peace.'

'Except for Zebedee,' she reminded him.

'Aye,' he muttered. 'He shames me, that one. I should have taken a stick to him when he was still a bairn, but your grandmother would never let me.'

'I knew my grandmother, but I couldn't love her,' Nell confessed. 'She was cruel to Ned and me. Was it because of what my father did to Zebedee? Did she guess who had made him lame? And did you?'

'Aye, we guessed,' said Grandfather McQueen. 'But, you see, I never blamed Albie the way your grandmother did. I knew my son.'

'Was he born wicked?' Nell asked tentatively.

'He was too clever,' the ghost said regretfully. 'He started meddling with the weather when he was six years old, by the time he was eight he could fill the house with little clouds, and when he was ten he blew the rain aside so that his mother could hang her washing out. But after his accident his talent turned into something evil. He would sit beside the window, glaring at the ocean as though the sea, itself, had maimed him. He used hateful, filthy language and only little Marina, your mother, could get close to him. If he ever loved anyone in this world, it was Marina; he never swore when she was near. But for the rest of us – I'll never know where he found such words; you'd think he'd invented obscenity, a boy of twelve.'

The fisherman cleared his throat with a drowning sort of gurgle. He gazed at his boots and wiped a hand across his face. He seemed to be making an effort to reveal something, yet couldn't decide if he should.

'Did it go on,' Nell coaxed, 'the swearing and the bad moods? Couldn't you stop it?'

'I tried,' the ghost told her sadly. 'One day I lost my patience. I gave that boy such a cuff it sent him sprawling on the floor, he bruised his chin and cut his lip but he didn't say a word. And then . . .'

'Then?' Nell urged, under her breath.

He gave such a sigh she could hear timbers breaking in it and a great hollow moaning wind that made her clutch at the chair for safety as she slowly knelt beside the ghost's wet boots.

'He limped down to the shore,' her grandfather murmured, 'and I never saw him again. It was a beautiful evening, the sky as bright as flowers, there was only a tiny hint of thunder, far, far away. So I took the boat out, thinking it was nothing. I saw no magic in the dark little clouds that scuttled towards me. I never dreamt that they were deadly.'

'Deadly?' said Nell through the wind that she could still hear creeping out of her grandfather.

'Aye, deadly,' he told her. 'They brought the storm that drowned me!'

'Oh, n-no!' she stammered. 'You can't mean . . . Zebedee?'

'I shall never know, lassie. Maybe he only meant to frighten me, and maybe it was real weather with no magic in it.'

'Maybe,' she said unhappily.

He leaned over, as though to console her, and the brilliance of his kind blue eyes brought Dylan vividly to mind.

'Is Dylan like his father?' Nell asked. 'He stole the crystals out of the sea. It seems he's just as bad.'

'No, lassie,' the ghost said reprovingly. 'You're mistaken. Dylan was only a bairn when he did that, a wonderful child who was obeying the man who made him what he was. You mustn't blame him.'

It was a relief to hear that her grandfather found no wickedness in Dylan, yet something still troubled Nell. 'Grandfather,' she said hesitantly, 'if you are not a kelpie, how do you know about the stories the crystals hold? How do you know about the valley of quartz?'

'That's where I am, lassie.' He spoke so quietly Nell

had to guess what he said. 'It's where I should be if Zebedee had left me in peace. It's my place now, child, that valley in the furthest ocean, and if I don't get back soon . . .' His troubled voice melted into the air.

Nell had almost forgotten he was a ghost. 'If you don't get back?' she prompted.

He turned his head from side to side, his desolate, weary features suddenly as real and precious to her as those of any living relative. And Nell knew that if there was a reason to anything then she was here to help her grandfather home.

'I'll take you back, Grandfather,' she said fervently. She had no idea how she would accomplish this, only that she must.

'I knew you would,' he breathed. 'And the crystals, Rainbow. Those too!'

'All of them?' She gazed at the brilliance of Zed's tower, thrusting into the dark.

'Your father will know how,' he said. 'Once before he tried to save me, but he was just a child then and didn't have the strength. Such a brave boy, he was. He set out all alone – I could see him coming, but the wind was too strong and sea like ice!'

'I don't know where my father is,' Nell said desperately.

'Then find him, lass, and soon.' His head drooped forward and he seemed to fade a little. A coolness, like a chilled hand, touched hers fleetingly.

Do ghosts need sleep? Nell wondered. She would certainly need it if she was to achieve the impossible.

'Goodnight, then,' she whispered and turned away from her motionless grandfather.

If she had looked back before she went into the house, she would have seen a slight figure move out of the shadows and go to the ghost in the wicker chair. But Nell was too engrossed in thoughts of her father. Just as she reached the staircase, however, she was sure she heard the fisherman murmur, 'There, child. You'll have a friend. She needs you, too, remember?'

NINE

Nell Tells a Story

In the early hours of the following morning an aeroplane droned over the island. Deep in sleep Nell had dreamed of home and foghorns in the bay outside her window. When she went downstairs, however, she discovered that her dream had led her astray.

'Dad's had to leave,' Menna told her. 'And Mum. They had an early breakfast and left two hours ago.'

'Why?' Nell asked, a little wave of panic sweeping over her.

'An emergency,' Menna said cheerfully. 'Mr Zed's business. Mum wanted us to go with them but Zed said there was no need, they'll be back tomorrow, and he and Delyth can look after us.'

Tomorrow seemed a long way off. 'Where are they going?' Nell asked, her panic beginning to show.

'I don't know. The mainland, I suppose,' Menna said indifferently. 'What's the matter with you? We can have a great time without those two wet blankets.'

Nell was rather shocked by this. She hardly knew what to say.

'They're so negative,' Menna explained. 'They always see too many problems to enjoy themselves. That's why Mum's gone along with Dad, to make sure he takes his insulin. He's diabetic, you see, amd Mum's always expecting the worst. She just can't trust him to look after himself.'

Dylan appeared beyond the pool, all in white, his hair as pale as his shirt. He gazed at Nell who looked away.

'What's happened between you two?' Menna asked.

'Yesterday you were conspirators one moment and enemies the next.'

'Nothing,' Nell said. 'At least . . .' She didn't know how to explain. 'It's just something I found out and . . .'

'And what?'

'And I don't know how to deal with it.'

'Try me,' said Menna in a conciliatory voice. 'I'm great at fixing things.'

I'm sure you are, Nell thought, but not in this situation. This is something that nobody ever dreamed of. My wicked uncle is an enchanter who is trying to steal the voice of the sea. He has made his son into a merboy and kidnapped his father's ghost. And now the ghost is so homesick his heart is breaking.

'What?' asked Menna, leaning over the breakfast table.

Nell was not aware of having voiced her thoughts. 'Nothing,' she mumbled, and then thought better of it. She needed help and Menna was all she had. 'I could tell you a story,' Nell said hesitantly, 'and then you could decide if you wanted to believe me.'

'Let's chat on the beach,' Menna said eagerly.

Nell glanced back at the breakfast laid so beautifully on a white cloth.

'Leave it,' Menna told her.

But thinking of Giselle, Nell piled silver dishes and ornate jam pots on to an empty tray, then slipping a roll into her pocket she followed Menna along the easy route to the beach.

'Don't go too fast,' Nell called. 'I lost you yesterday and got hijacked.'

'Oh, yeah?' Menna sang lightheartedly. 'We didn't get a ransom note.'

'He let me go eventually.'

'I suppose you mean Mr Zed. So that's why you were acting so strange. That man does look a bit like a hijacker, but why would he want you?' Menna sped past spearlike leaves of wicked green, waving her arms at giant rhododendrons as though none of Mr Zed's actions could shock her.

'I'll tell you,' Nell said, breathlessly pursuing Menna.

They whirled on through the shrubs in silence, while branches rustled grudgingly about them and there crept into the topmost leaves a little whistling sigh, that seemed to warn of breezes that might soon grow into something strong and deadly. And then they tumbled on to the beach of startling blond sand. It made the sea look bluer than the sky and Nell was reminded of a portrait of her true mother, Zebedee's sister, Marina, with eyes of *lapis lazuli*. The girl her aunt called Ultramarine.

Menna flung herself, laughing, into the sand. 'It's the most gorgeous place I've ever been,' she declared. 'You should have come yesterday.'

'I told you I was hijacked,' Nell said gravely.

'Of course!' Menna sat up. 'Tell all!'

Nell searched for a beginning. 'I suppose I'd better start when I was a baby,' she said.

'Is that entirely necessary?' Menna asked in mock gloom. 'I mean, eleven years ago?'

'It's when it happened,' Nell said impatiently. 'It won't make sense if I don't tell everything.'

'OK. OK.' Menna fell back and closed her eyes. 'Go on!'

Finding the pale eyelids and rigid limbs rather disconcerting, Nell turned her gaze on the sea and found the story unfolding more smoothly than she could have hoped. 'We were born on an island in the North Atlantic,' she began, 'my brother Ned and me. When I was a baby my real mother drowned and Ned, who was three, and I were taken from the island by our Uncle Dorian and Leah, his wife. Dorian was a good person and would have made a wonderful father, Leah says, but he had a brother who was quite the opposite. He was selfish and cruel and he had discovered how to call up ghosts when he was still a boy. His sister, my Aunt Rhoda, says they were all a little afraid of him. Well, when my mother died, Zebedee, the wicked brother said that he wanted us. I'm not sure why but Aunt Rhoda said he was terrible when he wanted something and couldn't have it, like a thunderstorm she said. But he was too sinful to be anyone's father, so she told Dorian to take us and drive down the coast away from Zebedee and his stormy temper, and not to stop for anything. But she quite forgot the dangerous winter weather and Dorian drove off the road and drowned in a place called Devil's Mouth. But we were saved, Ned and I; they found us on the beach "delivered on the morning tide," Leah says. "Safe on the sand." My brother dreams of this, sometimes, but I can only hear the ocean's footsteps. It always make me happy, this sound,' she glanced at Menna who was sitting up now and frowning at Nell. 'That's all,' Nell said with a hopeful smile.

'And I suppose you have just found out that Zed is Zebedee,' said Menna, who seemed to have fallen very eagerly into this history of magic and treachery.

'Yes,' Nell said, wondering how she could explain the kelpie if Menna asked.

Which of course she did. 'All that stuff is pretty amazing and I do believe you,' Menna said. 'Although I won't ask you how the ocean can have footsteps. What I should really like to know is where was your real father while all this was going on, and where is he now? I knew Mark was your stepfather but when your mother was drowning and one uncle was trying to save you and the other one was trying to steal you, why didn't your real father help? Did he abandon you?' Menna added her last question as though the thought had just occurred to her.

'Oh, no!' Nell said quickly. 'But he's always away. He lives at sea and . . . well, he's so busy saving things he hasn't got time to see us very often.' It was the truth

91

and yet it sounded wrong because Nell couldn't describe those joyful visits when her father returned with adventures humming out of him like music; the way his sea-eyes glistened, the salt on his lips and the tiny shells that hid in his bright hair and tumbled out like confetti when he gathered his children close.

'His name is Albie Nightingale,' Nell said quietly.

'Terrific name,' said Menna generously. 'So where is he now?'

'I don't know,' Nell whispered, almost afraid to let the words out because it was like admitting a silence into her head, where there should have been the steady throb of footsteps. She found herself running to the sea, ripping off her shoes and letting the water glitter across her bare feet. But even now, when she was in the ocean, Nell couldn't hear the footsteps. If only someone else were here; she thought, someone who knew what to do. She struggled to remember who it was that she wanted and managed a brief glimpse of her brother before long fingers, like a five-barred metal gate, banged shut across Ned's features. 'I believe Zed's trying to sweep Ned out of my head,' she said in astonishment.

'Were you talking to yourself or to the sea?' Menna had wandered to her side.

'I'm trying to think of my brother,' Nell said. 'He left Heathrow Airport for the Middle East on 1 August. My father was to meet him. There, I've remembered.'

'You are weird, Nell!'

'I'm not,' Nell cried. 'Oh, please don't think that, Menna. At school they say I'm weird, but it's only because I can't always concentrate. I'm listening for things, you see, behind their conversation. Oh, please don't give up on me, Menna!'

'Of course I won't,' said Menna steadily.

They both looked at the water and an ominous little wind moaned towards them over the waves.

'I think we're going to have a storm,' said Menna. 'Let's go back.'

They put on their shoes and ran into the trees. The wind began to whine, continuously, over the sand, but the sky was still a brilliant blue without a hint of grey in it. Nell thought she glimpsed a flash of white, just ahead of them, as they jogged along the path, and then she became certain that someone was moving beside them, deep in the wilderness. Menna was not so jaunty now and Nell wondered if she was a thoughtful person, after all. Did this small chatty girl really understand her?

'You didn't explain your quarrel with Dylan,' Menna reminded Nell.

'What about it?' Nell had almost forgotten how their conversation had begun.

'Are you afraid that he's like his father?' asked Menna.

Nell came to a halt. 'Yes,' she replied.

'That's silly.'

'Why?'

'They're hardly similar, are they?'

Nell had to admit that Menna was right. 'I suppose not,' she said.

'Dylan's harmless,' Menna told her. 'A hopeless case.'

For some reason Nell resented this description. Dylan was, after all, her cousin. 'Don't forget the swimming,' she said. 'That wasn't hopeless.'

'The swimming,' Menna said. 'Yes, well, that's another thing. Weird, really.'

Now out of breath, they paced wordlessly along the path until they came within sight of the house. 'I think I was a bit hasty,' Nell confessed. 'I was so frightened when I realized who Zed really was, I thought that maybe Dylan was part of the plot.'

'I doubt it,' Menna said amiably.

As they walked round the pool a scuffle in the shrubs caught their attention and, looking back, they both recognized Dylan's blond head, half concealed behind a clump of bright red fuchsia.

'He's been spying on us,' Menna said. 'I bet he heard every word. I thought there was someone in the woods.'

'He's been right behind us for ages,' Nell agreed.

'Eavesdroppers never hear good of themselves,' Menna loudly declared.

The fair head bobbed down and they heard him thrashing away from them, back towards the beach, and although Menna tugged Nell's arm, drawing her attention away from the boy, Nell still saw Dylan, in her mind's eye. She saw him reach the sand; she saw him rush into the water in his bleached white clothes, and swim far, far out into the wide blue sea.

'You've gone all glazed again,' Menna complained. 'Don't worry about him.' She sailed on up the verandah steps and into the shadowy hall.

'Wait,' called Nell, unaccountably anxious. 'Please, Menna.' She stumbled after her friend and plunged into the hall, only to be confronted by another solitary watcher.

The ghost sat, very rigid, in a tall hooded chair, his white hair ablaze, his luminous gaze transfixing Nell as she hovered on the brink of the shadows, with the warm sun still on her back.

'Now what is it?' Menna turned on the stair. 'You look as though you've seen a ghost.'

I have, Menna! Nell wanted to cry, but riveted by her grandfather's eyes, could only speak to him. 'I'm trying, Grandfather,' she said.

'What are you talking about?' Menna's down-to-earth voice disturbed the ghost. He beamed an irritated frown at her and Menna shivered slightly; she caught hold of the bannisters saying, weakly, 'What's going on?'

'It's my grandfather,' Nell said, still half in sunshine.

94

'Your grandfather?' Menna followed the direction of Nell's gaze. She scowled at the hooded chair in the dark corner. 'I'm fed up with you,' she said.

'Menna,' Nell said desperately. 'I know it's hard for you to believe, but there's a ghost sitting on that chair. It's my grandfather. His name is Alistair McQueen and he was drowned more than twenty years ago when his fishing boat went down in a storm. Now Zed has brought him back to explain the voices in the crystal tower. Him and me, we're the only ones who can do it, isn't that right, Grandfather?'

The ghost smiled approvingly.

Menna clung closer to the bannister. She seemed to be trying to shrink. Nell ploughed on. She had burned her boats; there was nothing to lose. If Menna thought her mad, so be it.

'But, you see, my grandfather wants to go home. I think he'll die if he doesn't. I know that sounds silly, but I can't explain it better. He wants to go back to the furthest ocean, beyond the islands where we were born, and he wants to take the crystals with him, as many as he can, because they don't belong here; they're part of a story that lives in the sea.' Nell said all this without taking her eyes off her grandfather; she dared not risk a look at Menna and yet she was aware of the small, rigid figure sinking slowly until she sat hunched on the bottom stair, her knees drawn under her chin.

During the wide, hollow silence that followed, Nell allowed herself a brief glance at Menna. The other girl was frowning at the air above Nell's head. She seemed almost too afraid to look at anything. 'You know you sound quite crazy, don't you?' Menna said at last.

'Yes.' Nell kicked unhappily at the tiled floor.

'So crazy that I suppose you must be telling the truth,' Menna went on, in a voice so grave and quiet that it was scarcely recognizable.

'Do you believe me, then?' Nell said hopefully.

'I suppose I do, but I'm not sure if I understand you.'

Menna looked fearfully into the corner where Alistair McQueen sat silently glimmering on his dark throne.

'Oh, Menna, I wish you could see him,' Nell said, happily. She ran to Menna, pulling to her feet. 'Come and meet him, please!' Then, to her grandfather. 'Help Menna to see you, Grandfather. Please try!'

The ghost turned his lightning-blue glaze on Menna. His eyes seemed so bright to Nell. She thought: Menna has to see his eyes, at least, and the half moon of his hair above them.

Alistair McQueen stood up, every second becoming taller and more definite, his determined weatherbeaten features emerging into the shadowy hall like a vivid portrait picked out by moonlight. Nell could even make out a darn in the cable of his thick woollen sweater, and a small tear in the corduroy trousers. She could see grains of sand caught in the wool and a callus on his knotted red hands.

'Do you see him, now?' Nell whispered.

Menna stepped closer, a little apprehensive but concentrating intently on the space where the ghost stood. Nell, her breath held tight in her chest, willed Menna to find her grandfather and to reach the mysterious butterfly touch of his hand. Her friend extended her arm and as the ghost's worn fingers closed over her's she exclaimed softly, 'I think . . .'

But even as she spoke a gust of furious energy burst about them. Alistair McQueen's bright eyes clouded and he began a dreadful sort of disintegration. Turning to the stairs he bent his arm across his face, as though shielding it from a deadly, dissolving ray.

TEN
The Albatross

The girls stood, petrified, gazing up the stairs while Zed looked down on them. He wore his frosty enchanter's coat, with the gems glittering like tiny flames about his wrists. His face was inscrutable. 'Well, girls,' he said. 'What are we playing today? A little game of make-believe? You must not meddle with the spirits, Nell.'

'You have,' Nell cried. 'And how dare you make him disappear like that? He's got a right to meet anyone he chooses.'

Menna gaped at her in unhappy confusion. 'What's happening?' she said huskily.

'Your friend is trying to play a trick on you, Menna,' said Zed. 'She's become a little unhinged.' He tapped his head. 'Poor child; it's why I invited her here. A sort of convalescence.'

'How can you . . . say that?' Fear broke Nell's sentence apart, she struggled to keep Menna's attention. 'He's lying . . . remember . . . I told you who . . .' The sparkling circle of gems twisted her thoughts, melting her speech into a string of ragged sounds. 'What are you doing to me?' she tried to say, but managed only a desperate croak.

'Run into the sunshine, Menna,' Zed told her. 'Take a swim and while you're about it, find my son. I want to talk to Rainbow, here.'

'Rainbow?' Menna frowned. 'You said that once before.'

'Didn't she tell you? Tch! Yes, she's a Rainbow and her brother is called Albatross, like his father.' He spoke the last word through a monstrous grin.

'Please don't leave me with . . .' Nell tried to speak, but Menna slid past her and raced into the sun without a backward glance. Nell couldn't blame her.

Above her, Zed beckoned with long dark fingers.

'Grandfather . . .' Nell pleaded.

If the ghost was near she couldn't see him. She couldn't even feel a friendly drift of air. She found herself approaching the stairs and compelled to mount them, one by one, until she stood two steps below the enchanter. He turned, walked up the second flight and along a corridor that led in an opposite direction to her room. And Nell followed with a weary tread, slouching in his footsteps like a slave on an invisible chain.

At last they reached a room that held a view of the shore. Nell could see the beach where she had been standing only moments ago. Zed must have been watching her, marking her out as she travelled the track through the trees with Menna. Perhaps he had seen his son's flight and knew that he had plunged into the sea.

Zed seated himself behind a wide mahogany desk. There was only one object on its gleaming surface – the necklace Albie Nightingale had given to his daughter. Nell gazed at it in angry silence.

'Yes, it's yours, Rainbow,' he said. 'But I needed it.'

Nell heaved a furious sigh.

'What right had I?' he answered her accusing glare. 'I borrowed it, Rainbow. I want to know what it says. I want to know it all, you see, every scrap of evidence that can tell me how the world began, and then I'll be the master, won't I? But it won't talk to me!' He tried to mask his impatience with a smile but only succeeded in looking more dangerous. 'I'm going to dig into the furthest ocean,' he went on with frightening serenity, 'and find every crystal in the sea.' Zed touched the tiny fragment of quartz caught on Nell's strand of gold and she could hear its call, as light as a bird's heartbeat. She had never heard its voice before, but then she had never listened.

Nell fought to find a voice, but her objections emerged as a pathetic mutter.

Zed laid his closed right fist on the desk, palm upward, and slowly uncurled his fingers, as though he were releasing some tiny fragile creature, and Nell felt words slide into her throat.

'How did you do that?' she asked, surprised to find he had not changed her voice into a frog's croak or a chicken's cackle.

'Practice,' he said and, leaning towards her, dropped the necklace over her head with such a benevolent smile, she found it hard to stay angry.

'Why do you need me?' Nell asked, clasping the necklace for reassurance. 'I can't translate the crystals for you. Bits of a story are no good without a beginning and you'll never find that if you blow up the ocean. Please let me go home!'

He glared at her, pressing his fists together so hard that his knuckles stood out as white as dead men's bones. The spears of light from his jewelled sleeves seemed to reach behind her eyes giving her a headache, and, all at once, Nell became fed up and very angry with his magic. 'You can't keep me, you know!' she said. 'I don't belong to you, just because you're my uncle.'

'My dear Nell, I'm practically the only blood-relation you've got. And you're quite wrong. I'm perfectly entitled to keep you.' He spoke with such crisp satisfaction Nell was terrified of believing him and giving up the struggle.

'Where's my grandfather?' she demanded. 'What have you done with him?'

'Oh, he's about,' Zed shrugged. 'Looking for his grandson, no doubt. But he can't go far without me.' He sounded as though he were speaking of some surplus relation who had wandered off to feed the birds, not a ghost who should be spoken of with respect.

Nell tried another tactic. 'I can't help you, really I

99

can't,' she said. 'I'm just a girl who can feel the thoughts of creatures that you will never, never understand.'

'What must I do to understand?' He made himself look so sincere she could almost see beyond the mirrors of his dark eyes.

'Take the crystals back to the furthest ocean,' she said earnestly. 'You won't learn anything from them. It's like stealing a leopard's coat or the horn from a white rhino. We've got everything, us humans. We don't need the ocean's secrets.'

'But it's knowledge, Nell,' he said relentlessly. 'Isn't that of value?'

'Not if you blast the ocean apart and rob it of its last treasure. Think of the creatures that will die. Things that we don't even know about.'

'What about archaeologists. Isn't their work worthwhile?'

'Why can't you understand?' Nell tried to thump the desk but managed only a feeble tap. 'They're not stealing memories,' her words were now spun out in whispers as she became aware of what she was saying. 'The crystals are alive, you see. They are in pain, the ones you stole, because they are lost.'

'And this?' He touched the necklace. 'Is Albie Nightingale not guilty, then?'

Nell couldn't immediately answer this. Perhaps her father was more human than he cared to admit. 'He took them for his wife and daughter,' she said reluctantly, 'before he really knew what they were.'

'He knew all right,' Zed said harshly. 'I'm tired of arguments, Rainbow Nightingale. I've released your voice so that you can tell me what I want to know.'

'And you won't listen to what you ought to know,' she said, quietly stubborn.

He stormed to the window, his lame foot hissing over the floor like an angry python. And there he stood, an outraged sorcerer, against the magical silver of the sea, until he saw something that enthralled him, causing him to press so close to the windowpane, Nell thought that he would surely burst through it. Following his gaze she found a rock not far from the shore, defined by a ring of surf. A bird appeared to have settled there; a huge white bird with a long rounded beak. Nell had never seen such a bird before but knew, instinctively, what it was.

'Albatross,' Zed murmured elatedly. 'Have you called your father, Nell?'

'How could I?' she said shakily. 'I don't know where he is.'

'I think you do, Rainbow. I think you do. The Albatross tells me that he's coming closer.' A deep and oddly gleeful sound broke from him and then he cried, 'Damn! Where's my son?' He whirled round, moved rapidly behind her and opened the door. 'You'll stay here until you promise to tell me what I want,' he said. But he spoke in a distracted way and it seemed that something far more important than Nell now needed his attention. When he had closed the door behind him, she heard a light click in the lock, and felt like something a spider had wrapped up, for future use.

Nell ran to the door and, as she expected, found that she had been locked in. She banged on the door without any real hope of being heard, then retreated to the window to find that only someone in the trees or on the beach would see her. The verandah, the pool and all the other inhabited parts of the island were out of sight. And who was there to see her, anyway? Only Menna, and what could she and Menna do, just the two of them on an island where Zed was master.

How did it happen? Nell wondered, sinking into a voluminous leather chair. How had Zed stolen her so easily from the safety of her happy home with Leah and Mark and Ned? How was it that growing older had made life so dangerous; one step leading into another until here she was, alone and miles away from everyone she loved?

101

She tried to fight a wave of drowsiness, but at last gave in to it. When she woke up she found that a lunch tray had been placed just inside the door. She had missed her chance. How long had she been asleep? The sun was dipping below the sea and the sky was patched with dark clouds.

She ran her fingers absently along the string of bright and mysterious shells, closing her eyes against a wave of tears. When she opened them, two great wings were spread over the thin line of the horizon. They loomed huge against the sky and then swung inland towards the house, and Nell's heart thundered as the albatross sailed right above her, its cry haunting every corner of Zed's island until it echoed with a hundred mysterious sounds.

Without knowing how or why she had left the chair. Nell found herself circling the room, trying to match the bird's call, over and over, finding notes in her voice that had never been used, cadences that she couldn't recognize. She didn't know how long she persisted in this strange song but it must have reached some far corner of the house for, eventually, a key was turned and the door flung open. Delyth stood staring in, breathlessly supporting herself on the door frame.

'What on earth are you doing here?' she asked.

'He locked me in,' Nell said defiantly.

'Zed?' Delyth inquired.

'Who else?' Nell said. 'He's mad, you know. Wicked and mad.'

'Don't be ridiculous, Nell.' Delyth looked away a little guiltily. 'Besides, he didn't lock you in. The key's still in the door.'

'Well, then, he forgot to take it with him. And I'm not ridiculous. I want to know when my aunt and uncle are coming back. I want to go home.' Against her will, Nell found that her voice was rising hysterically.

'Calm down,' Delyth said uncomfortably. 'Anne and John will be back soon, but not tonight. Our pilot won't fly in bad weather unless it's absolutely necessary.'

'Bad weather?' Nell remembered the ominous little gust of wind that had crept over the sea. She turned to the window and saw that during her wild bird calls, clouds had gathered in the distance; huge clouds tipped with orange, that boiled over the horizon in frightening and unnatural formations. The trees that had been rocking quietly were now in a turmoil and the sea looked dark and dangerous.

'He did it,' Nell said. 'He can steal voices and conjure up dead fishermen. You can't pretend you don't know, you're his wife.'

'Yes, I'm his wife,' Delyth said flatly, 'and that's all. Zed is a very clever man, but someone has frightened you with stories of hocus-pocus. You can't begin to understand his talents.'

'And nor can you,' Nell muttered, but Delyth was frowning at the window and Nell saw a dingy-looking boat with a rattling motor, not far from the shore. Probably a fishing-trawler Nell thought, and of no help to me. But then a small rowing-boat was lowered into the sea; someone climbed into the boat, perhaps two people, Nell couldn't be sure, but now it was pulling away from the trawler and seemed to be heading towards the island.

'Fishermen,' Delyth observed. 'What do they want?'

Whoever they were, they were from the outside world. Nell raced past the puzzled woman with a little cry of hope, and bounded down the stairs, two at a time, thinking, I'll scream if I have to, but I'll make them help me, somehow.

Outside the air was definitely cooler. Every plant and tree was shivering in the unexpectedly chilly wind. The verandah and the terrace were deserted. Not even the grandfather's blue eyes peeped through the icy gusts. Had Zed banished him for ever?

From the woodland track she could see Menna standing forlornly by the sea while Zebedee paced the tideline, restlessly, one arm pointed, imperiously, over the water. When Menna saw Nell she ran to her, giving her a hug that squeezed her breath away.

'What's happening?' Menna cried. 'Mum and Dad won't be back tomorrow, after all, Zed says. There's a storm coming. I'm scared, Nell.'

'Did you call those fishermen?' Nell asked, breaking free of the hug but still clasping Menna's hand for comfort.

'I just waved,' Menna told her. 'I didn't mean any harm. They must have thought we needed help, because of the gale warning. They were only trying to be kind. But all at once, Mr Zed came whirling out of nowhere with his terrible limp, and yells, "Go away. We don't need you. Get back before the storm swallows the lot of you." Oh, Nell, he's mad with me. What's he going to do?'

Nell, looking past Menna, saw the small boat pull away, and as it departed over the dark swell of the sea, the man on the beach turned away from it, to watch the girls. And Nell found the scream she'd wanted to use had all dried up. She couldn't even lift an arm to beckon the fishermen back.

'An albatross has come,' Nell whispered. 'So we mustn't give up hope.'

ELEVEN

Enchanter's Weather

Still holding hands Nell and Menna backed away from the enchanter, but they couldn't break free of the hooded gaze until they reached the trees and then they ran; ran, almost sobbing for breath, along the track to Zed's cool white house.

Even there they didn't stop but pelted past an astonished Delyth and up the stairs to Nell's room where they slammed the door and threw themselves on Nell's pink bed, gasping for air and drawing each other further into terror with their wide frightened eyes and dreadfully exaggerated grimacing.

'Oh, Menna,' groaned Nell, 'I'm sorry but you look almost funny. I think we're more scared than we need be. He can't hurt us!'

'What d'you bet?' said Menna. 'People who are mad can do anything.'

'He's not mad,' Nell told her. 'He knows very well what he's doing. And I won't be scared of him. I just won't!' She was almost enjoying herself, she realized. 'I've dragged you into this,' she went on, 'and I'll get you out!'

Somehow their roles had been reversed. Nell had never imagined that she would be the stronger one, or that she would find herself comforting Menna.

'What was all that about an albatross?' Menna sat up, trying to be resolute.

'I'm not really sure,' said Nell, momentarily baffled. 'But it has something to do with my father. It's his name, you see, Albatross, and the bird has suddenly come out of nowhere.' She saw again the huge wings that had covered her view of the sea; embracing wings, downy soft beneath the long feathers. 'I think it's a sort of messenger,' she said.

Menna frowned hard at Nell. 'Did you leave something out,' she said, 'when you told that story about Zebedee trying to steal you when you were a baby?'

'It's not easy to tell everything at once,' Nell said. 'If I kept something back it was because I badly wanted you to believe it. My past is so unusual, I have to be very careful about who I choose to know it, and how and when to talk about it.'

'How about now?' demanded Menna. 'I think I deserve some sort of explanation. After all, it seems that I've been caught up in a very peculiar and, maybe, even dangerous situation.' She looked intently at Nell. 'And you must admit that, up to now, I've tried to listen and tried to understand.'

Nell, looking at her friend's earnest face, decided that the time for truth might never be better. It didn't seem fair that Menna should find herself all alone in the midst of a strange and sometimes violent family. 'I once tried to tell you about kelpies,' she reminded Menna.

'Yes,' Menna slowly agreed. 'It had something to do with that necklace you're wearing. Why are you wearing it, come to that?'

'It doesn't matter,' Nell said. 'I'm trying to tell you about my father. You know I said that people thought kelpies stole young women and maliciously drowned them, well I think they took them for love and didn't drown them but taught them how to understand the ocean, so that their children were born with thoughts that were fed by the sea, and they can't survive without it.' In giving this explanation, Nell was beginning to enlighten herself.

'Perhaps there is a meaning to all this that I should understand,' said Menna helplessly. 'But I don't. I was never very good at English Comprehension.'

Nell took a breath and said quickly, 'My father was part kelpie. At least that's what he told us, and anyway it explains the way we are, Ned and me.'

Menna shifted her position. She sat on her hands looking embarrassed and Nell was afraid that, after all, she had chosen the wrong person to confide in. 'It's true, Menna,' she gently persisted. 'That's why I can hear the crystals. They come from the furthest ocean, like this one on my necklace, and they hold memories; memories of plants and creatures that we'll never know about. But they belong in the furthest ocean with the rest of their story; they're lost out here, built into Zed's tower.'

'Oh,' said Menna. She was clearly struggling to understand. Menna was not a girl who enjoyed fairytales; she had always preferred true stories about people who were nice and ordinary and had adventures that were surprising but not impossible. At last a grave sort of amazement stole into her face and she said, quietly, 'I'm glad you told me. Of course, I'll never be able to tell anyone else, but I do believe you. I'm going to keep your secret like you keep a treasure, and when I'm bored or lonely, which isn't often, I'll remember what you said and think about it for a while, and it'll make me feel . . . it'll make me feel happy in a completely different way.'

Nell did not know how to respond. She was so profoundly relieved, and so grateful to hear Menna's words she could only give her a small, but very sincere, smile. Perhaps I have found the best friend I could ever have, she thought.

Someone knocked on the door and without waiting for an answer, Giselle looked in. She appeared to be agitated. 'Mr Zed would like you to come for supper now, ladies,' she said and, after a hesitation, added, 'There's a storm coming on and I don't like the feel of it.'

'Are you scared, Giselle?' asked Nell.

'Don't you like thunder?' asked Menna. 'Or lightning?'

'I don't like them, but I'm not scared of them,' said Giselle a little indignantly. 'This storm is different, though.'

'Different?' Nell enquired.

'Don't ask me how. It just is.' Giselle retreated, leaving her words like lethal little parcels, dropped at their door.

'Is she trying to frighten us?' wondered Menna.

'No. It's Zebedee's storm,' Nell said slowly. 'He can conjure the weather.'

'Oh, come on,' Menna said nervously. 'People can't change the weather.'

'Zebedee can,' Nell told her. 'But we won't let it frighten us. We'll put on our best clothes and act like princesses who are out to conquer the world.'

'It's getting cold,' Menna said doubtfully. 'I think I'd feel better in a sweater. Has Zed given you anything warm to wear?'

Nell searched the drawers and found a woollen tunic with silk stars decorating the collar and cuffs.

Menna sighed enviously. 'It seems he's thought of everything,' she said. 'Perhaps living with him wouldn't be so bad?'

Nell shook her head. 'The trick must be to wear his clothes without letting them change me into someone I don't want to be!'

'But, Nell, they have changed you,' said Menna quietly. She went to change and brush her hair and when Nell met her, five minutes later, outside her room, she looked a little more like the cheerful girl who had bounced into Nell's home, only three days ago.

As they approached the dining room a sinister whine could be heard above the rattle of the long windows and raindrops tapped the panes like insistent, bony fingers. The storm was almost upon them.

Zed seemed to have forgiven Menna her foolish

behaviour over the fishermen. He had even, conveniently, forgotten that Nell had been locked up for half the day. Now he was in a buoyant mood. He found the boisterous weather promising. Taking his place at the head of the table he indicated that Nell and Menna should sit on either side of him. Delyth was already seated in the chair beside Menna and Nell was delighted to find that her grandfather had come to join them. But he looked isolated and rather frail, at the far end of the table. There was no sign of Dylan.

'Have you seen my son?' Zed asked Nell, and she detected a note of concern.

'How could I?' she returned. 'I've been locked up for hours.'

'Nonsense, girl,' he chided affectionately. 'You fell asleep. By the way, my love,' he said to Delyth, 'Rainbow here is a long-lost relative.'

'So I hear,' Delyth said wearily. 'Why couldn't you trust me, Zed, to know your family secrets?'

'It was to be a wonderful surprise,' Zed told her cheerfully.

'It was a shock!' Delyth looked accusingly at Nell and began to serve cold soup into four delicate white bowls. The fifth remained empty.

'Delyth, where is Dylan?' asked Zed.

She shrugged and began to sip the cold *vichyssoise* daintily from the tip of her spoon. 'You know he doesn't always eat the meals that Pierre prepares,' she said. 'Unless it's seafood, of course. If you had provided a bucket of krill I'm sure you'd find him here.'

'He's your son,' Zed continued, as though he hadn't heard her. 'You ought to know where he is.'

'My son,' Delyth gave a choked little laugh. 'Oh no, Zed. He might be yours but I don't know anything about him. You've made Dylan a mystery to me.' She laid her spoon carefully in her bowl and pressed a starched white napkin to her lips. 'He's probably hiding in the house somewhere, you know he does,' she said.

'He enjoys the effect it has on you.'

Nell wondered if she should tell them that her strange mind's eye had seen Dylan plunge into the sea, hours and hours ago. She decided to keep it to herself. After all her mind's eye might not be reliable.

'As long as he's safe,' Zed murmured, hunching his shoulders under an invisible cloak and faint thunder rolled, achingly, about the house. 'Do you like my weather?' he asked, turning to Menna.

'Yours?' she said in a small voice.

'Mine,' he said proudly. 'I have just about perfected my thunder.'

Menna gazed unhappily at Nell.

'You don't believe me, do you, child?' laughed Zed. 'Listen, then!' And he raised his arms, drawing a moan of wind into the room that pulled their hair across their faces, sent all the place-mats fluttering and made the glasses tinkle like a charming little orchestra. 'There!' he said.

Menna sucked in her lower lip. She seemed ready to cry and Nell burst out, 'You're not to do this, you bully. I won't have you making my friend miserable.'

'But she still doesn't believe me, Rainbow,' he said plaintively. 'And I can do so much more.'

Glaring at his son, Alistair McQueen stood up. He fought to speak but only a distant cry crept out of him. The whole room silently called Zed to stop, but he could not. He hadn't enjoyed himself so much for years, and the encroaching storm only served to bolster his vibrant, wicked energy. Smiling, he pointed one finger at the ceiling and a little flurry of snow blossomed round the lantern. It fell gently over Menna, covering her head and shoulders with tiny stars of ice.

Menna gazed at the snowflakes in horrified fascination while Delyth leapt to her feet, crying, 'Zed! Don't do this, please. I beg you!' as though his wonderful show was closing a door on her that she would never be able to open.

110

Before Zed could answer his wife something swooped through the storm outside and beat on the windowpane. Surprised by Zed's silence, Nell glanced at him and saw that he was staring at the window with an extraordinary expression of dread and anticipation. 'Ah . . .' he muttered.

'It was a bird,' said Menna, glad of the distraction. 'A huge bird with wings like . . .' She spread her arms.

'An albatross,' Zed told them.

'I thought they belonged in the South Atlantic,' Delyth said, 'and never ventured north of the Equator.'

'Oh, they do! They do!' Zed clasped his hands together and the crackle of gems at his wrists sent a tiny spark shooting across the table. A thread of lightning blazed through the dark sky and a thunderclap rocked every candle on the table.

TWELVE
Zebedee's Wife

'Enough!' growled the ghost. 'I know what you are doing, Zebedee!'

'What's that, Father!' asked Zebedee, too pleased with himself to ignore his father any longer.

'You can hear me, boy,' wheezed the ghost.

'Yes, I can hear you!' The enchanter glared down the table, past the silver candlesticks and a vase of tall white flowers. 'But no one else can; except Rainbow, of course.'

'Is there really a ghost in here?' asked Menna, scanning the room with wary excitement.

'I'll have to admit there is,' said Zebedee complaisantly. 'My niece wasn't playing a trick. I've called my father back to help with . .'

'Stop it!' Delyth commanded. 'I won't have it. There isn't a ghost in my house. There never was and there never will be.'

'Oh, Delyth,' sighed her husband. 'I can see I'll have to prove it to you.' He rang a tiny bell placed, like a wine glass, beside his plate and Giselle arrived, in a second, at his side. 'Fill a glass and take it to my father,' he told her.

Without a glimmer of surprise Giselle obediently filled a shining wine glass almost to the brim with deep red wine.

'Giselle has never doubted me, you see,' said Zebedee, looking at his wife. 'I'm sorry it's not whisky, Father, but wine suits my purpose better. The colour is more obvious.'

Indifferent to the varying expressions of horror and

112

amazement directed at her, Giselle walked calmly towards the ghost. She held the glass at eye-level, as though it were a brew of priceless, magical potency and she had sworn, on pain of death, not to spill a single drop. And although she could not see the fisherman, she set the glass directly beside his hand, then moved away to watch him drink.

She must have practised that, Nell thought.

'I will not do it, Zebedee,' muttered the ghost. 'I will not frighten your good wife.'

'Cheers, Father,' said Zebedee and he raised his glass with a scornful laugh.

'You evil boy. You never cared for anything or anyone!' the ghost accused.

This caught Zebedee off guard. A little of his arrogance began to slip away, leaving his face surprisingly grave. 'I had a little sister, once,' he said quietly, 'but the kelpie drowned her. And once I had two good legs that could outrun the fastest hare, now I cannot run at all. And there's Dylan . . .'

Alistair McQueen gazed sorrowfully at his son. 'Zebedee, what has become of you?' he said.

They both seemed to have retreated to their small chilly home beside the wild white sea, where family battles raged around a twelve-year-old boy with eyes so dark they might have been burned into his face.

The grown-up Zed cupped his chin in his hands and curled his fingers, like a flower, round his face. The jewels on his cuffs sent spiralling silver light across his hawk-like features, but he spoke like an ill-tempered boy. 'You never appreciated me,' he complained. 'Don't you realize that I'm amazing?'

'You're a monster,' said his father.

'Be quiet!' yelled the enchanter, leaping out of his pensive mood. 'Drink your wine or I'll banish you. I'll send you where you won't even see your grandchildren, where no one can find you. Where no one can save you or take you home.'

113

A silent battle raged across the table. The ghost refusing to obey his son, determined not to frighten anyone. The air between them shuddered and the white flowers, caught in a furious draught of conflict, suddenly dropped all their petals.

'Oh,' breathed Menna, 'is it a poltergeist?'

'It's willpower, girl,' Zed snapped without losing a moment's concentration.

Gradually the gentle fisherman was overcome. He regarded his glass of ruby wine with great sadness and lifted it reluctantly to his lips. Menna watched enthalled while Delyth turned her head, very slightly, but enough to see the glass raised and the wine tipped into nowhere. 'Zed?' she cried. 'Why are you doing this?'

'My love,' he said with gentle wickedness. 'I want you to understand me. You approve my practical skills and enjoy the advantages my cleverness brings you, but you refuse to believe in my "other" talents. Why, won't you, dear?'

'I don't want to,' she said grimly. 'I hate what you have done to our son and I can't live with a ghost.'

'Tch!' Zed shrugged impatiently. 'He doesn't bother you. And where *is* Dylan, incidentally? This hide-and-seek has gone on long enough.' He limped to the window and gazed on the havoc his storm had brought to the garden: the pool stained brown with leaves and petals, and the paths a jumble of twigs and broken terracotta. And Nell found herself seeing in the tall enchanter another man, made quite ordinary for a moment, by a tiny ache of love.

'He went to the beach,' she heard herself saying, in a voice that frightened her with its quiver of alarm.

'The beach?' He spun round and stared at her in disbelief. 'When?'

'Ages ago, before the fishermen came.'

'I haven't seen him all day,' Menna put in timidly.

'All day? All day?' exclaimed Zebedee.

They watched him pace before the windows, afraid

114

for him and for themselves until Nell burst out, 'I thought you knew. He was all in white. You couldn't miss him.'

'He wasn't dressed for a swim then?' Delyth said hopefully.

'No. But he did go swimming all the same,' Nell said.

'Nonsense.' Delyth pursed her lips.

'Be quiet,' her husband told her. 'Rainbow says he went swimming.'

'Rainbow!' Delyth bleated. 'Why can't you call her an ordinary name?'

'Because she is extraordinary,' Zed said tersely. 'What makes you say that my son went into the sea?' he asked Nell.

'I can't explain,' she said wildly. 'But you know that I see things, like a picture made out of sounds, in my head. Dylan ran into the water. I felt him do it.'

'Why? Why did you feel my son run into the water, Rainbow? Why?' His face loomed over her, hungrily, and she had to lean away from it.

'Because I'm close to him,' Nell said, all at once realizing what that meant. 'Because he's kin, like you, only he's not like you at all, although you tried to make him. The sea has soaked any wickedness out of him. I know that now.'

The words that came bounding out of Nell seemed to throw the enchanter into an extraordinary state of confusion. He gazed at her fearfully and yet with a deep and yearning affection, and then he swung himself away and rushed into the hall, calling, 'Pierre, the boat! We must launch the boat immediately.'

From a distance Pierre protested, 'No, Mr Zed. In this weather it would be madness.'

'Do as I say,' roared his master, limping out into the wind.

He left them in a room still resounding with his panic and throwing them together in their alarm and bewilderment.

115

For the first time Delyth spoke to Nell as though she were not her enemy. 'It can't have been easy,' she said, 'being part of that family.'

'Interesting though,' amended Menna, trying to look courageous. 'Never dull!'

Nell smiled thankfully.

'It's been very hard for me,' said Delyth, through something like a sob. 'Living with . . .' She avoided the word enchanter, it wasn't in her vocabulary. 'My own son, too,' she murmured tragically. 'Perhaps I haven't tried hard enough to understand.'

'I think you should treat Dylan as just an ordinary boy who can do something wonderful,' Nell said gravely, 'for that's what he is, just a boy. He'd get closer to you if you'd let him.'

Delyth looked at her in sudden surprise saying, 'I believe you're right. Forgive me, Nell, for my – hostility!'

'You couldn't help it,' Nell said, smiling forgiveness at the woman she longed to help.

Outside a flash of lightning swooped across the clouds and thunder crashed above the roof like an explosion. 'What if they don't find him?' Delyth cried. 'Is he really in the sea?'

'Dylan won't drown,' Nell said. 'Water is like air to him, he'll let the ocean carry him. And, anyway, if Zed has conjured up this storm, he can stop it if he wants to.'

'Nooooo!' boomed the ghost. 'It's gone too far for that,' and he swayed towards them, cutting through the room like a gust of glacial air. The enchanter had momentarily, forgotten him and Grandfather McQueen was on the loose, sweeping boldly into the atmosphere with all the strength he had used to try and keep his life. And Nell knew that Delyth and Menna must see him now, with his dazzling tumble of hair and brilliant truthful eyes.

116

'What is it, Grandfather?' she cried. 'How has it gone too far?'

'He could never control his temper,' boomed the fisherman. 'It's going to get worse.'

Nell didn't understand. She looked at Menna and Delyth. Without a doubt they had seen the ghost. Delyth had chosen to hide from him and covered her face with her hands, but Menna was gazing at him through frightened tears. 'Going to get worse?' she whispered.

Nell couldn't say a word. Something distracted her. An empty space in her head had begun to fill with distant footsteps.

'I can't help it,' Menna said. 'I'm not exactly scared but I'm worried for Mum and Dad. I miss them a bit more than I thought I would, and I've got this awful feeling that . . .' a stifled sob escaped her, 'that I'll never see them again. Maybe we'll be surrounded by ghosts and storms forever.'

'It's going to be all right,' Nell said, running to Menna. 'My father's coming.' And she beamed on her friend the joyful smile that came from knowing that Albie Nightingale was near. The footsteps were getting clearer, they rang in her head like music from her heart.

'How d'you know your father's coming?' Menna said, more upset than cross. 'All of a sudden you know. Well, where's your private radio, your walkie-talkie, your cordless telephone? Or have you got a crystal ball?'

'Don't be cross,' Nell said with sympathy. 'Just believe me!'

But Alistair McQueen had looked into the past. 'Of course he's coming,' he said and his voice rose above the long-ago moan and rumble of a drowning boat. 'It's what Zebedee wanted all along. The crystals were only a part of the game. Perhaps he does want to know how the world began, but more than anything he wants Albie Nightingale. He knew he'd come for you, lass.

117

The albatross found you and now your father is following the bird into the storm that Zebedee has drawn about you.'

'Me?' Nell said, suddenly feeling small and baffled. Delyth was watching her, outside the scene but wanting to break into it. 'Won't he stop for anything?' Nell asked desperately. 'Not even Dylan. You can tell he cares about him. Won't he calm the waves a little, just enough to launch a boat?'

'I'm not sure, lass,' said her grandfather. 'Zebedee is crazy with success. He wants to show your father that, at last, he's stronger. That he can win!'

'Then we're caught,' cried Menna, talking directly to the ghost. 'If Albie Nightingale can't break through the storm, who can?'

'Who says he can't,' Nell said hotly. She ran from the room across the hall and through the doors that led on to the verandah, while Menna and Delyth called, 'Nell! Nell! Nell!' The doors had crashed heavily behind her and she found that she couldn't pull them together against the wind that screamed into the house.

'Nell, you mustn't . . .' Delyth cried, but the rest of her sentence was scrambled by the jangle of breaking glass and the whine of Menna's frantic voice shouting, 'Delyth, please stay! I can't be here alone. I can't!'

Nell wasn't at all sure where she was going or why. She was responding instinctively to the call of the ocean, knowing that Albie Nightingale was drawing closer. She could feel her grandfather behind her, but as they moved away from the house his bulky figure seemed to wither into a stream of flying leaves that was swept up by the wind. Zebedee had filled the weather with so much malicious energy that nothing could stop it, least of all the man who had invited it. And Nell began to wonder if, after all, Dylan could survive a storm of mountainous waves and furious lightning.

At the top of the island the crystal tower blinked in the rain and a little tide of excited whispers reached

Nell. They, too, could feel Albie Nightingale's approach. Someone was coming to save them.

I'll offer him my knowledge, Nell thought. I'll tell the enchanter anything he wants. I'll tell him I'll stay with him forever, and hope that he can't read my thoughts. But I must make him break the storm so that Albie Nightingale can sail through and save us all.

She had no doubt that Zebedee was in his tower, now. Where else should be be? From his sky-high attic over the ocean, he could watch the water with his sharp hawk-eyes. Nell tried to run towards the tower but found that her feet were caught by the wind, in invisible waves of stone. She pushed against it, her head bowed against the rain and the lightning that illuminated the horizon without interval. Fighting for breath she gradually made her way across the howling field, and only once did it occur to her that she could be shrivelled to carbon or bowled clean off the island. But this fear came fleetingly, like a small burr, caught in the flesh of someone who had a mountain to conquer.

Nell had to crawl the last few metres over the rock to the glittering tower. The tall building was moving with the wind and the whispering had become intense. Too exhausted to reach for the circle of shells that would open the door, Nell took shelter beside the tower, kneeling as close as she could to the tiny daggers of light. They welcomed her with a fluttering excitement. Their tone seemed to have changed entirely, their sadness replaced with joyful expectation.

Nell laid her cheek against the crystals and there was a hesitation in their voices, as though they were arranging their words in a pattern that would please her. When they spoke again their rhythm matched the soft footsteps in her head.

'He's very close,' Nell shouted through the wind. 'Albie Nightingale is coming to save us. No one can stop him.'

The voices responded. They whirled through Nell in

cadences that she could translate. The music became creatures of unbelievable beauty, creatures whose colour stunned her and whose touch made her gasp with wonder.

Still holding fast to the tower Nell eased herself round to face the wind that blew in from the sea. And there it was; a tiny fleck on the heaving water; it could have been the crest of a wave but she knew that it was not. It was *The Dolphin*, its sails lashed down tight, its pennant glittering with salt and the painted silver dolphin on the prow, leaping through the mountainous water as though it were a real creature, flying for joy.

Nell had to get closer. She tore away from the tower and raced down the path to the beach. But where there had once been a wide stretch of sand there was now only a strip of pebbles lashed by waves that rose ten metres high. No one could land a boat in such furious water. And then Nell remembered the first time she and Ned had seen their father. Three years ago the spring equinox had brought a record stormy tide to the coast. The giant breakers had drowned islands, torn cliffs away and swallowed half a town, but Albie Nightingale had come to them, on a soaring column of silver water so high they believed he had to be Neptune or a trick of moonlight on water. And now he would ride the waves again, she knew he could. She was not quite sure, however, that he could steer *The Dolphin*, or even a dinghy, close to the beach.

She moved along the narrow strand of pebbles trying to get a glimpse of the boat, but now that she had left the cliff-top, she had lost sight of it. A nervous apprehension gripped Nell. There was no boat. She had seen only what she wanted to see. *The Dolphin* was a mirage, conjured up by the enchanter to give her hope. But the whispers stole through her panic, telling her to look again, past the towering banks of water, beyond the driving foam, to a boat, tiny in the distance and as fragile-looking as a bird, persisting in its journey through the waves.

Nell shrank against the cliff as a torrent of water plunged towards her, taking the boat out of her sight. And, as she turned her face away from the stinging spray, she found her eyes gliding up the rainswept pillar of stars to where a dark shadow moved within its crystal walls. The enchanter was harnessing his spells, every straggling loose end of magic that he had ever learned was being gathered into his angry mind to hurl at Albie Nightingale.

Bracing herself against the wet cliff Nell waited for the shudder of the next wave, but it never came. A deep and deadly calm fell over the ocean, smothering the waves into silent ripples. The wind dropped and *The Dolphin* swept in towards the shore; when it reached the path of rainbow-coloured lights that Zebedee's tower cast over the water, Nell held her breath. She could not believe that the enchanter had given up the fight.

He had not. Beyond *The Dolphin* a black cloud circled the water. Slowly it grew into a whirling column veined with shining and intense blue. It danced behind the boat like a frenzied human echo, its arms raised high, ready to smother; a giant waterspout of murderous electricity, charged with all the power and all the hate that Zebedee could muster.

'Look behind,' Nell tried to shout, but not a word escaped her. The boat could not have turned, anyway. It was lost. The deadly column of water was only seconds behind it. Albie Nightingale had seen his daughter, he raised an arm and then someone appeared on the deck beside him; someone much smaller with a head of pale gold hair.

'Dylan,' Nell murmured. She looked up at the enchanter's shadow, unmoving in his crystal shell. Had he seen his son? And if so, would it alter his intention?

'Zebedee!' Nell cried. 'Please! It's me, Rainbow! Let

121

them go and I'll tell you what the crystals say. I'll even stay with you. But don't . . .'

He couldn't hear her. The column of water whirled relentlessly onwards. Albie Nightingale had seen it now. He faced the tower of gleaming water and the boat tilted as the first shock waves hit it. Nell sank speechless on to the rocks. She was about to cover her face when the waterspout suddenly spun away from the boat. For a moment it wheeled aimlessly, a twist of glittering energy with nowhere to go; then, all at once, it lurched towards the shore, gathering speed as it went, almost, it seemed, as though intent upon a victim. It moaned like a creature in pain as it drove into the crystal tower.

A fountain of stars flew a mile into the air. Tiny, scattered voices called from the sky and then the shells and stones and shining quartz fell into the sea. For a moment the ocean blazed as bright as the moon and every wave was tipped with silver. Then the crystals dropped to the ocean floor and their voices were lost in the water. Behind them threads of sparkling light marbled the surface of the sea and Nell thought she had never seen anything more beautiful or more desolate.

She was quite alone.

The tower had vanished and so had the boat. The rain had turned to an icy drizzle and Nell, wet and cold, clung to hard rock, like the only person left in the world.

THIRTEEN

Losing the Rainbow

Nell tried to wish it all away; the water and the cold and the dying crystal stars. She closed her eyes and pressed her cheek against the cold rock, telling herself that when she woke up she would find that the day was just beginning, and it would be quite different from the day she had just imagined.

But the truth was colder and sharper than the rock and she couldn't escape it. She gazed at the ocean through tears that might have been her own or wind-blown seawater; and then she saw them! Two figures were scrambling on to the rocks far down the shore. Nell ran towards them, slipping on seaweed and wet rocks, grazing her knees and her hands. When she reached her father her fingers were laced with little streams of blood. But she felt no pain as she was lifted off her feet by the strongest, wildest man in the world.

They swung together, so close they might have been one, and when Nell was set on her feet again a silky blond creature peered round her father and said, 'Hullo, cousin!'

She had never seen anyone so wet, his skin was gleaming and his thick pale hair shone like a mirror. Nell found herself giggling hysterically. Dylan looked so funny and so alive.

'This young fellow popped out of the water like a seal,' her father told her. 'He introduced himself and convinced me that my efforts to reach you were not good enough.'

'Where's Ned?' Nell asked, suddenly searching the

123

sea, afraid that her father's smile might be hiding something.

'I left him behind, Nell,' he said. 'Ned is becoming an expert in cleaning oiled birds. I'm proud of him. And, as you know, they need all the help they can get.'

'I'm sorry to call you away,' Nell said. 'I couldn't help myself.'

'I know!' Her father hugged her.

They climbed the cliff path and when they reached the barren rock where the crystal tower had blazed into the sky, they found there was nothing left but broken shells and a thin dusting of quartz that sparkled like frost. Dylan emerged, last of the three. He hadn't realized that his father's tower had vanished entirely and stood motionless, balanced at the very edge of the cliff and in danger of tumbling back into the sea.

'Dylan,' Nell said gently. 'I think he saved you.'

'What?' His voice was distant.

'Your father,' Nell said. 'I think he saw you and turned the waterspout away.'

'He was in the tower,' Dylan gazed at the drift of crystals, 'then . . .'

Albie Nightingale took his hand, drawing him into safety. 'He could be anywhere,' he said. 'We'll search.' But Nell knew that her father was using words of comfort without any real conviction.

They walked to the house in silence, Dylan moving like a sleepwalker. The wind had died completely and when the clouds rolled away from the island, they left a heavy warmth behind them, and a huge amber moon.

Every window in the house was ablaze with candlelight, and Menna ran out to greet them crying, 'Did you see it? An explosion of stars like the end of the world.'

'The tower's gone,' Nell told her.

'Gone?' said Menna in disbelief.

'The storm took it,' Nell said, she didn't know how to describe the dreadful column of electrified water.

'And Mr Zed?'

Nell shrugged, 'We don't know. He was in the tower.'

'In the tower?' said Menna, caught between horror and relief; but she wasn't a girl who could dwell too long on mysteries and was already intrigued by the tall stranger at Nell's side. 'Is this your father, Nell?' she asked shyly.

'Yes,' said Nell, proud of her father but sad that the enchanter's disappearance caused nothing more than brief excitement. Standing close to Albie Nightingale Nell felt small and safe and yet part of her yearned for the bold rainbow that Mr Zed had found in her. Would she lose it now?

Albie Nightingale was shaking Menna's hand. 'Are you a member of the family?' he asked. 'You must forgive me but I'm seldom on dry land and I lose track of relations.'

'I'm a sort of cousin,' said Menna who looked as though she wished she could claim a closer relationship with this splendid adventurer. She took him into the hall beneath a candelabra whose glimmering light showed Zebedee's possessions at their best; the glowing tapestries and rugs, the dark and ancient furniture leading to wide marble stairs, and Albie Nightingale paused a moment, dazzled, turning his head this way and that, bewildered by all the magnificence set down in the middle of the wild Atlantic. Perhaps he was comparing it to his own home on a damp and creaking boat.

'Zebedee has done well for himself,' he said a little wistfully.

'You have the ocean,' said Dylan, who was anxiously scanning the hall. 'Where's my mother?' he asked Menna.

'Upstairs,' she told him. 'She was acting kind of funny; lighting everything as if she expected guests, or maybe warning someone. For a moment I thought she

125

wanted to make a bonfire in the house.'

Nell was watching Dylan. He had taken off his wet shoes and outsized oilskins and was making his way across the hall. When he reached the stairs he stopped and gazed upwards with an expression of dread.

'Dylan,' Nell ran to his side. 'Do you want me to come with you?'

He frowned and said, 'I think it's something I have to do by myself.'

'Your father might be . . .' Nell faltered and turned to Albie Nightingale. 'He could have left the tower before it fell, couldn't he?'

'Anything is possible,' her father said.

Dylan smiled wanly. 'Was my mother worried about me?' he asked.

'Of course,' Nell said. 'We all were, especially Zed.'

Dylan nodded slowly. 'I had to show him that he was wrong,' he said. 'I had to use the skills he taught me to find your father. Although,' he turned to Albie Nightingale and added ruefully, 'it seems you would have found Nell anyway.'

'No, Dylan,' the adventurer said solemnly. 'Without you I might have lost the battle. Your father's storm was overwhelming me. He's very powerful.'

'Yes,' Dylan agreed and, all at once, he touched Nell's hand. 'I think I would like you to come with me,' he said. 'I don't know how I'm going to tell her.'

As Nell followed him Dylan quickened his pace, mounting the stairs more forcefully and when he reached the top, almost rushed along the corridor to his mother's room, his face set in funny determined lines like someone who was afraid of losing their concentration. And Nell began to worry in case his mother didn't care how he felt, and wouldn't understand why he had swum out to find Albie Nightingale. She would be very angry with the bearer of such terrible news. She might even hate Dylan for it.

126

Delyth's door was open and she was standing by the window, staring out at the night sky. An oil-lamp glowed on the chest beside her and a white moth hovered round it.

'Mum,' Dylan began and then realized that his mother knew everything. She had seen the crystals fly and guessed the rest. But when she looked round at him she seemed stunned but not tearful. If there was any expression at all on her face, it was one of relief. She ran and hugged her son as though she would never let him go.

Nell closed the door and left them. She began to walk back along the corridor and then, overcome by a dreadful weariness, she leant against the wall and sank slowly on to the floor. Without knowing why, she began to cry. Huge, breathtaking sobs spilled out of her. She tried to close her mouth against the sound and folded her arms tight across the ache in her heart. She told herself there was nothing to cry about. Everyone was safe and Dylan had a mother who cared about him after all. And then she knew that she was crying for herself, and for the dark enchanter who, for a short time, had made her into a rainbow.

Her father approached her carefully, his bare feet treading the carpet like a panther. He squatted beside Nell and felt her wet hair. 'What is it, little one?' he asked.

For a moment Nell's sobs made it impossible for her to answer, but eventually, with a deep swallow, she blurted out the truth. 'He made me into a rainbow,' she said. 'No one ever saw me like that. They thought I didn't want to be noticed. They saw me as a dreary person, who was afraid of adventure and didn't take part in things. I know Zebedee had a wicked heart but he saw me as someone special, someone he wanted with him – always. But you . . .' she broke off with a cry, pressing her fists against her mouth. 'Oh, I'm sorry,' she gasped.

'Who called you Rainbow?' her father asked softly. 'Who knew as soon as you were born, that you were so very special you had to have a name that reflected all the colours in the world.'

'You did.' She glanced at him, almost shyly.

'And you know why you can't be with me – always?'

She nodded beginning to feel ashamed of her outburst.

'You are as important to me as every bird and every creature in the ocean,' he told her. 'But you are a member of the human race, Rainbow. You have privileges that they do not. Someone has to fight for them.'

'I know,' she whispered, wondering where her voice had gone. 'I think I have been the victim of a very clever spell.' And looking into the sea-coloured eyes and the mischievous smile, Nell knew that she would not have exchanged all the bright clothes, all the sunshine and adventure for just one visit from a father like Albie Nightingale.

Alone downstairs, Menna wondered what the two strange Nightingales had found to laugh about.

When Delyth and her son appeared, Delyth seemed almost too composed. She had re-applied her make-up very carefully and changed into a plain dark dress. It was as though she had ordered her wardrobe and rehearsed her lines for this very occasion.

'I must radio the mainland,' she said calmly. 'I don't suppose they will do anything tonight, but Zed was an important man. There are people who are bound to want details of what happened. I expect the police will mount a search. Launches and helicopters, that sort of thing. And the material, the crystals I should say, his associates will want those.'

'The crystals are going home,' Nell said.

'Home?' Delyth said with a frown.

'To the furthest ocean,' Nell continued firmly. 'It's where they belong.'

'We'll see.' Delyth did not want an argument. However, she wasn't going to be deprived of what she considered was rightly hers. 'They're worth a great deal of money, I believe.' She spoke quickly and then whisked herself away through a door beneath the stairs, where her husband kept his radio transmitter.

'I'll explain,' Dylan said. 'I think I can make her understand.'

They went to the kitchen to find the food and hot drinks that suddenly seemed necessary in this strange damp weather. A saucepan of pasta had been left to boil dry and the long table was piled with unwashed pans and greasy crockery. They remembered poor Pierre had been ordered to launch the motor-boat, and realized that Giselle had probably gone out in the storm to search for him.

'We should try to find them,' said Albie Nightingale.

Nell followed her father on to the verandah, and they gazed out at the island, unable to decide where to start, or if there was any point in searching for a boat that had been in such a turbulent sea.

'The Dolphin,' Nell said suddenly. 'What happened to her?'

'Broken, I'm afraid,' her father told her, 'but not lost. She's drifted into the bay beyond the tower.'

And then two figures stumbled into the light thrown out by the lamps and candles set in almost every window. Nell knew they had to be Giselle and Pierre but they were almost unrecognizable. Dazed and bedraggled they lurched forward looking like survivors of the worst sort of disaster. Albie and Nell helped them into the house where they clung together, soaking wet and barely able to talk. Delyth brought them hot tea and huge white towels and gently rubbed Giselle's mane of gleaming hair while Pierre began to talk in helpless rambling sentences.

They learned that Zebedee had not climbed into the motor-boat with Pierre. He had helped to launch it and

129

then told Pierre to steer round the island, observing every cove and inlet to see if Dylan had been stranded somewhere by the high sea. Zebedee himself had gone up the tower, from where he expected to get a broad view of the ocean.

The sea had become a battlefield of currents and the wind spat electricity. Pierre became convinced that the lightning was seeking him out and that every second brought him closer to a horrifying end. He also had the gravest suspicion that Mr Zed was orchestrating the weather.

'He was looking for a boat,' Pierre grunted. 'There was someone on that boat he wanted; I believe it was a man he'd been searching for all his life; the man who was responsible for this,' he tapped his leg. 'He told me once that this man was not completely human.' Pierre glanced furtively at Albie Nightingale who threw back his head and laughed.

How wonderfully her father hid the truth, Nell thought.

'Mr Zed was a proud man,' Pierre went on a little resentfully. 'But his lameness prevented him from being perfect. It was, how do you say, a flaw, and it went deep inside.' He laid his hand over his heart. 'You understand?'

'But in the end he sacrificed himself,' Nell said quietly.

'You think so?' Pierre said hopefully, and it seemed to Nell that the question, spoken with such genuine innocence, hid all too many meanings. Had the enchanter really controlled that deadly column of water? And if he had, why had he allowed something he'd invented to overtake him? Was he really gone?

'The children are looking tired,' Delyth remarked. 'They need sleep.'

The children did not deny this. They ambled up the stairs, murmuring 'Goodnight' to their relations and each other, and leaving the adults to chew the events into rags if they wanted. Nell, Menna, and Dylan could not take anything more into their aching heads.

FOURTEEN
Waiting for the Fisherman

A police-launch arrived very early next morning. The sea was like a sheet of glass, and a helicopter rattled in the blue sky. Wherever Zebedee had gone, he had taken his murderous storm with him.

There were two passengers on board the launch; Anne and John Parry, who welcomed their daughter with such a display of emotion, Nell was sure her friend would flee from it. But when Menna released herself, at last, she didn't even look embarrassed. Perhaps, after all, she preferred her safe and steady life to Nell's topsy-turvy one.

Three athletic-looking men in uniform surveyed the tumble of shells and crystals; all that remained of Mr Zed's pillar of stars. Far below them, the ocean glowed, as though lit from beneath by mysterious moonbeams.

'What is this?' asked the tallest of the three policemen. He looked older than the other two, and in a position of authority. He had introduced himself as Inspector Doyle.

'It's quartz,' Delyth replied a little haughtily.

'Strange,' he said. 'It seems to have a light that is, how do you say, not entirely a reflection but comes from inside, like there is a little flame in there,' and he pushed at the glittering splinters with his foot, as though he were nudging a wounded animal. And Nell almost cried out, for she could hear the voices, calling to each other like lost children.

'We'll continue the search for a while,' the inspector addressed himself to Delyth, 'but it looks hopeless. I am sorry but if we don't find anything in the next hour or so . . .' he shrugged and turned his palms to face the sky.

'I understand,' Delyth said quickly. 'When you leave I'll come with you, if I may. There will be things to attend to on the mainland. My husband's affairs were rather complicated. I'll have to see the bank and . . .' for the first time her speech faltered and she could only murmur, in a helpless way, 'My husband was a powerful man, you know.'

'I do. Mr Zed was not unknown to us,' said the inspector. His smile did not seem entirely sympathetic and it occurred to Nell that the law and Mr Zed had not always seen eye to eye. 'We will, of course, take you back, and anyone else who wishes to leave the island,' he said.

'We have our own boat,' said Albie Nightingale, laying a hand on Nell's shoulder. 'It was damaged in the storm but I'm used to that. It'll soon be as good as new.'

All three policemen now looked at Albie, their expressions wavering between uneasiness and respect. They didn't know quite what to make of this unusual-looking man. There was something about him they could not identify; something that would never be captured in small black notebooks.

'I'm sure you're right, Mr . . .' the inspector hesitated.

'Nightingale,' said Albie with an engaging smile and added, rather recklessly, 'Albatross!'

'Ah, yes,' Inspector Doyle cleared his throat, avoiding Albie's penetrating sea-blue eyes.

Dylan, who had been gazing at the crystals, suddenly came to life. 'I'll have to stay,' he said to his mother.

'Darling,' Delyth said gently. 'If your father isn't found, then it means . . .' she tossed her head, trying to shake herself free of the choking sob that had crept into her throat, 'he's not coming back!'

'It's not that,' said Dylan, looking earnestly into his

133

mother's unhappy face. 'I want to come with you, Mum, you know I do. But I can't, not yet.' He looked round, frantically, for someone who might help him to explain, and found Nell. 'I want to stay with Nell.'

And Nell, reading his thoughts, pleaded, 'Let Dylan stay, Aunt Delyth, please! I'll have no one to talk to when Menna goes, my father will be working on the boat all day.'

As the three policemen walked away from family matters, Nell stared at her aunt, not daring to let her mouth frame the words, but silently forcing Delyth to understand what neither she nor Dylan could explain aloud. That he was waiting for a ghost.

'Let him stay,' said Albie, interpreting the silent message. 'Just for a while, Delyth. I'll take good care of him. You'll have so much to do, so many people to meet, you'll scarcely have time to see your son. And, after all, it seems that I'm his uncle.'

'You're right,' Delyth said quietly. 'I'm being selfish. I know that he'll be safe with you.' She did not ask herself how she knew this, it was something she had understood, instinctively, as soon as she saw Albie Nightingale. 'But don't keep him away from me too long,' she begged, and Nell knew that whatever Dylan did, his mother would never reject him again. He had, very quickly, replaced the fierce and clever man who might have been her husband but had always remained a stranger.

Giselle and Pierre decided to accompany Zed's wife to the mainland. Without the man who had run their lives, they couldn't stay, they said.

Before the police-launch took everyone away, Nell spent an hour writing letters. Even though the Parrys had promised to telephone Leah and assure her that Nell was safe with her father, Nell had so much to tell she knew that only a letter would do. First she wrote to Leah and Mark, telling them she was happier than she'd ever been, that she had found a cousin and would be sailing, at last, with her father. But she did not mention Grandfather McQueen. To Ned she wrote a very simple message because some of the things she wanted to say could not be put on paper. 'I have made a friend,' she wrote, 'and found an uncle and a cousin, but now the uncle has vanished. I have also met Grandfather McQueen. I know he would like to have seen you but we must take him to the furthest ocean. I will tell you all about him very soon.' She addressed the letter, 'care of Olof Pehrsson'. Olof was a friend of Albie's and keeping an eye on Ned.

Menna said she would put the letters in the very first post-box she saw, and that she would run to it in case she missed the collection.

It was the quietest evening Nell could remember. She and Menna had parted friends forever, sworn to write constantly and to see each other every holiday. But Nell was glad that just the three of them remained. The ghost would feel more at ease among people who loved him dearly.

Albie Nightingale was sitting on the verandah, lost in a voyage among the stars, seeking in the sky a route to the furthest ocean. He hardly noticed the children walking away from him in search of their grandfather.

'Where shall we look?' said Dylan. 'He might be hurt or confused by the things that have been happening, and afraid to come back to us.'

'We'll go to . . .' Nell was about to say, 'the tower,' but seeing the starless void above the trees, said instead, 'We'll go to where he might have been when the tower fell.'

As they approached the barren slab of rock, where the pillar of stars had reached into the sky, Nell began to wonder if they were waiting for someone who had never really been with them at all; perhaps they had imagined him because they had been lonely and afraid.

'Has it occurred to you,' she asked Dylan softly, 'that

135

he might have gone with your father into the sea, and will never now come back?'

'No!' said Dylan passionately. 'Our grandfather is here, somewhere, but now Zed's gone he's been set adrift, somehow, like a person with bad eyesight who can't focus properly. I *know* he'll come back. Without us he can't get home.'

They had reached the forlorn stretch of broken, glittering quartz and Nell felt compelled to kneel and stroke the sharp fragments that called to her so piteously. And she found herself gathering them up by the handful and pouring them into her skirt where it had billowed on the ground.

'You'd better leave them here, where they're together,' Dylan advised in a very mature voice. 'Tomorrow we'll find them all and when my grandfather turns up, we'll take them to the furthest ocean.'

'But they're lost in the sea,' Nell reminded him. 'We'll never find every one.'

'We will,' he told her firmly. 'I found them and I shall take them back. Every tiny piece.'

Nell was immensely impressed by this determined and forthright boy. For an instant, she wondered if a part of Zebedee had sneaked back to hide in his son.

'Will you miss him very much?' she asked.

He knew immediately whom she meant. 'Of course, I will,' he said. 'But Nell, I don't think he has really gone.'

The light was fading very fast and the crystals had begun to take on their own fierce glow. Nell let them slide gently off her skirt and then she stood up to try and read his face. 'Not gone?' she asked.

Dylan gave her a mysterious smile. 'Let's go back,' he said, 'and wait for our grandfather near the house. It's getting spooky out here.'

'A spook is what we're looking for,' Nell told him with half a grin.

They ran back, just managing to overcome a fit of nervous giggling before they came within sight of the house. Albie had not moved from his chair and still seemed to be contemplating the peaceful, dark blue heavens.

Nell and Dylan knelt beside the pool and became absolutely silent. When an orange moon seemed to set the water on fire they didn't move. And when a shooting star fell across the island they didn't even speak of it. They hoped that if they were as still and silent as stone, their hearts might stop beating for a moment, and trick the air into thinking they were two ghosts, and bring a third to join them.

Albie Nightingale began to feel the children's silence. He could barely make them out against the bright glimmer of water. They were moving, now, like a single shadow, deep violet in the midnight air, and beginning to approach him. As they drew near they began to drift apart and he knew that someone he couldn't see was with them, holding their hands.

Nell's father got out of his chair and walked down the verandah steps. He waited for the children and when they stood before him he shaded his eyes and observed a cloud of moonlit dust circling between them. And then a voice he recognized, called to him from what seemed like a long way off in time and place, 'Help me, Albie Nightingale!'

And he remembered the man he had tried to save when he'd been just a boy. 'This time I *will*,' he said. 'I promise you, Alistair McQueen!'

FIFTEEN

The Furthest Ocean

Dylan began to dive before sunrise. When Nell reached the rock at eight o'clock the treasures he had trawled were already heaped in small, glittering pyramids beside the ocean. He carried the crystals in a leather bag that Albie Nightingale had provided.

The swimmer would not talk to Nell but continued to work until midday, his face without any expression, diving into the clear deep water, with his eyes wide open and his hair drifting round his head like a plume of pale feathers. From the rock above he could hardly be discerned from the tricks of sunlight on submerged rocks, or the graceful crowds of fish that now and again rippled round him.

At sunset Dylan assured them that he had gleaned every particle of crystal from the ocean floor. 'There's nothing left,' he said. 'I'm sure of it.'

They poured the quartz into four large canvas sacks that Albie, once again, produced from his locker on *The Dolphin*. Nothing but natural fibres ever reached his boat. It seemed strange that all the tower's magic sparkle was now contained in just four canvas sacks. For they had decided to take only the crystals, leaving the shells and coloured stones to decorate the beach and, perhaps, surprise a stranger who, one day, might alight on the enchanter's island. The concrete blocks had tumbled into the sea and the wrought-iron staircase lay twisted on the beach.

'Shall we go tonight?' Nell asked her father. 'Now that everything is ready.'

'At first light tomorrow,' he told her. 'I like to start a journey in the dawn.'

So they were to spend just one more night on Zed's island and, for Nell, it was to become a night filled with dreams so strange and yet so vivid she would carry them in her head always. She would never be quite sure if she had been wide awake and glimpsed, through half-closed eyes, an enchanter who stole about her room like a blue velvet breeze. He had touched the gifts he had given her, the bright clothes and glass animals, the golden-haired bear on her pillow and the slippers set with coloured beads. And under his long fingers each object had sparkled as though dusted with sunlight. The enchanter had waited for Nell to compliment him for his splendid magic and, puzzled by her indifference, he had covered her bed with a blanket of flowers, but still she could give him no sign of wonder or approval. Then, with a moan that seemed to have been dredged from the end of the world, he raised a hand encircled by fiery gems and described an arc in the air above her bed, and with great care and precision he had filled the arc with bands of colour until a rainbow grew inside her room, brighter and more perfect than any she had seen on a rainy day at home. But still Nell couldn't tell him that he was wonderful and astonishing, although she tried to. And so, spent with sorcery, the enchanter had limped from her room and she had listened, sadly, to his lame foot whispering down the passage like a despondent, weary serpent.

When she opened her eyes and found that her throat allowed familiar sounds to escape from her, she was cross with herself for being unable to speak to her night visitor, and then she told herself that she must have been asleep. 'You've been dreaming, silly!' she said.

But did she believe herself? For on the floor, just at the edge of a white rug, a rosy-coloured jewel blinked in a frail shaft of light.

Nell swung slowly out of bed. She picked up the tiny gem and put on her beaded slippers that were now, she noted, quite free of their magic look. Then she took the jewel downstairs to look at it in the garden, and found Dylan sitting on the steps of the verandah. He looked as though he hadn't been to bed at all.

'This was in my room,' Nell said, holding out the jewel.

Dylan took it from her. He let it roll around his palm for a moment and then he tucked it into a pocket.

'Will you come back here?' Nell asked.

'I don't know if Mum will want to,' he said, 'but I shall. And I think I'll try and find Pierre and Giselle and ask them to live here so that when he . . .' he broke off and stared hard at Nell, daring her to ask him what he meant, or finish the sentence for him.

'So that he'll be with friends?' she suggested.

Dylan smiled. 'Do you think you'll come with me?' he asked, looking intently at her. 'Will you dare?'

After her night of dreams she didn't know how she would answer this but, all at once, she found herself saying, 'Yes, I will, because like you, I don't think I can really let go of it forever.'

Nell's father had moored the repaired *Dolphin* at the end of the jetty and after an early breakfast they stocked the boat with provisions from the house, stowed the crystals in the cabin and cast off. It was perfect sailing weather: a light wind from the south, a calm sea and a cloudless sky.

Alistair McQueen had been waiting for them, he was already on the deck, his brilliant blue eyes eagerly scanning the northern horizon.

As they whirled away from the ivory beach Nell saw Dylan casting a deep reflective gaze at the island behind him, as though he were pondering some painful enigma whose solution was gradually escaping him.

To Nell, Zed's island looked entirely peaceful and it

was difficult to believe that anything frightening or unusual had happened there. And yet she knew from the strangely altered rhythm in the way she spoke and moved that she had been enchanted, and that the spell had changed her forever. She was a more definite self; sure of her decisions, proud of her unusual family and happy with the way she looked. Even her feet looked more positive and this made her laugh. Dylan, following her gaze, laughed with her, for in her haste to scramble aboard she had put her shoes on the wrong feet.

For a week they sailed in endless blue and, during that time, Dylan and Nell began to learn how to sail around the world, for Albie Nightingale taught them almost everything he knew. They learned to find their position with a sextant and the sun, how to read their direction in the stars, how to take the sail in and when to let it out. They even learned to drink coffee with powdered milk and to eat hard biscuits instead of bread, and because the sea was already in their blood they learned fast and were never ill.

Sometime during the second week a change occurred in the weather. Nightfall began to edge away until it hardly seemed to come at all, a dark sea rolled heavily around them, the breeze dropped and one morning they woke to find themselves rocking in a never-land of mist. Progress became very slow. Once or twice they had to use precious fuel and motor out of the fog, seeking a wind to fill the sails. At night they couldn't sleep because of the crashing of the gear above them on the deck. And then they entered weather with a bite in it and Nell knew they were somewhere near the island where she'd been born. She could tell from the way her father gazed eastward every day, with a puzzled yearning on his face.

'Yes, they're there, somewhere,' Albie said, close to Nell's ear, 'the islands where your mother lived. We'll visit them on our return, though the house where you

141

were born has been swallowed by the sea.'

'I know,' Nell said. 'I wish Ned were with us.'

It was then that a whale, the length of a ship, surfaced beyond them, and blew a fountain of silvery spray at the sky. The size and wonder of him put all Nell's sad thoughts to flight, and left her gasping with delight. And for the first time during their long voyage Alistair McQueen spoke; it was scarcely more than a murmur of contentment but it made him seem a little more substantial. Reminded of his mission, Albie Nightingale quickly steered *The Dolphin* into a wind that would take them north again.

Soon they were into wild weather. There was ice in the wind and the sail froze stiff as an oak door. The children were given outsized coats with sheep's wool linings, thick woollen hats and mittens lined with fur, and still their cheeks froze and their teeth chattered. Sometimes the heaving sea would wash right over them, soaking them to the bone and they would spend a day below decks, trying to dry out. Albie began to look for baby icebergs that might sneak up on his precious *Dolphin* and smash into her hull. Whenever a fishing ship hove into view he would call her on his radio, asking for news of the weather ahead.

And then, one day, there was nothing; nothing but freezing fog and a rolling icy sea. No wind at all. They hardly moved for three days, but on the third night the fog cleared and they could see the full moon and a sky crackling with stars. And there, reaching for the moon, a mountain of ice, four hundred metres long.

'Is it land?' Nell asked in a whisper.

'It's an iceberg,' her father told her. 'It has come from the frozen Arctic where it has lived for millions of years. Perhaps no man has ever seen it until now. It is going south to meet the warm Atlantic where it will die.'

They gazed at the shining mountain of ice, savouring the thought that they might be the only people in the world to have seen it at its most splendid and Albie said quietly, 'I think it is time to turn back.'

The children stared at him in horror. 'We can't,' they both said.

'Listen,' he commanded. 'The food is getting low, the fuel is almost gone. The pack ice is ahead of us. I dare not risk your lives by going any further.'

'But our grandfather,' Nell said.

The ghost was standing in the stern with his back to them. His feet were planted firmly on the deck and his wild hair was as startling as the iceberg.

'We have to take him home,' she insisted.

Her father did not speak. He rested one hand, anxiously, on the wheel. She had never seen him look so uncertain, or so lonely.

'You promised,' Dylan said, in a hushed fierce voice.

'And the crystals,' Nell added, but her heart flew out to her father, who found himself, perhaps, for the first time in his life, without a solution.

'Is it really too far?' Nell asked dismally.

For what seemed a very long time no words at all were spoken on *The Dolphin*. The boat rocked gently and the iceberg drifted away to its melting death. It was surrounded by a flotilla of smaller bergs that danced and bobbed like frantic children playing a last game before bed.

Now there was nothing between the boat and the horizon except a vast moonlit ocean. They never knew who saw it first but it was Dylan who said, 'It isn't moonlight.' And really they should have noticed sooner for moonlight doesn't burn so fiercely that it makes the air shudder with its brilliance.

A wonderful smile lit Albie Nightingale's stern face and placing both hands on the wheel he swung *The Dolphin* into the wind. It flew towards the furthest ocean like a homing bird and Alistair McQueen came striding back, his boots riding the lurching deck like a true fisherman. He dropped down between the

143

children and took their hands. 'Hold fast,' he said. 'We're going home.'

They had taken off their mittens and could really feel his hands, strong and warm and heavy. They held on, very tight, with their faces bathed in the ancient and utterly mysterious light, until their grandfather began to slip through their fingers, and they were left with only the damp wind between them and a pale crest of hair that might have been seaspray.

'The crystals, children,' Nell's father said urgently.

The sacks had already been brought on deck and now the children leapt into action. While Albie held the boat steady they poured the glittering fragments into the sea. The crystals whispered ecstatically as they tumbled into the water and Nell and her father heard the ocean of stories welcome her lost children with a great hymn of joy.

Before Albie Nightingale turned *The Dolphin* away, he waited a moment so that Dylan might listen to the oldest voice in the world. Even if it was only a fragile chiming in the boy's head, Albie wanted him to hear the sound, for it was too beautiful to be missed.